TANGLED DECEIT

VEILED VENGEANCE BOOK TWO

HEATHER RENEE

HARPER REED

CONTENTS

1

OLIVIA

Being captured by a mafia leader even once shouldn't be something most people worry about in their lifetime. Let alone having it happen twice.

Unless you're me, of course.

Even worse was finding out that the father who abandoned me all those years ago wasn't just some asshole guy who couldn't hang around for the hard stuff. He's been living the mafia life, trying to be a king. Which means he's decided to try to take down Luca and...who the hell knows what else.

All I know for sure is that Titan and I might be tied together by blood, but he's no family of mine. Not after he kidnapped me and put me in a room without so much as an "I'm sorry I left you."

Do I find it funny that I'm in pretty much the exact same situation I was in just a few weeks ago? Mildly, but

I'm not the same woman I was that first day Luca tossed me into his cell.

I'm stronger, both physically and mentally, after surviving being thrown into this insane world, being attacked, and even allowing myself to fall for Luca. While there have been times over the years that I've missed my father, like when he could have taught me to ride a bike or attended my graduation, he doesn't have a hold on me. Not now that I've seen him in this setting.

Titan, as he'll now be known to me—not Dad or Christopher as I thought he went by—spent the car ride from Luca's to wherever we are now in silence. The "little chat" he suggested we have doesn't seem to be a priority for him, because after I felt I had no other option than to get in the SUV with him, the only other words I heard him utter were a cold command to his men. "Bind her."

Dread had filled me at first, but now, I'm drawing on my anger and motivation to get the hell out of here as soon as I find the opening I need.

Since we began driving, I've been blindfolded and had my hands tied together behind my back. Knowing that I'm going to need my strength for the perfect moment when I stand the highest chance of escaping, I haven't fought back. Yet.

I let them easily restrain me. I haven't asked any questions or even begged for them to let me go. When someone picked me up out of the SUV after we got to this place, I didn't even try to headbutt the fucker who held me, even while I hated that his arms weren't Luca's.

Now, I'm sitting in a chair, ignoring the ache in my shoulders from having my arms pinned behind me and trying to pretend that a new itch isn't popping up on my face every other minute.

Time passes, but I have no idea how long it's been since I've been left alone. I don't know if there's anyone in the room with me or if they're watching me through a window. Regardless of all that, I keep as much emotion from my face as possible, even when my worry about Luca begins to surface or whether he might be able to find me.

I won't give anything away to Titan. He won't break me.

For the first time since I received the news of my mother's death, I'm grateful she isn't alive. Her heart never healed from being left without a word. If she knew the truth...that just might have killed her anyway.

A noise breaks the silence, the soft twist of a doorknob. My heart races as I fight the urge to tense up. I won't be afraid of this man. I've been dodging death since the moment I walked away from that charity auction. If it's my time to die, then so be it. I won't go easily. Though, I also have no intention of giving this bastard the pleasure of hearing me beg for mercy just because his DNA runs through me.

A chair across from me scrapes against the floor, and someone settles into it with a thud as the room begins to fill with the scent of musk and cigars. I'm pretty sure a palm or two thump onto the table I'm certain is in front of me. Even though I can't see it with my own eyes, I hear the sound of fingers tapping on a solid surface.

"You've grown into quite the woman, Olivia," Titan's voice breaks the silence, and a shiver runs down my spine. Memories of a distant childhood flicker in my mind, of a man who was supposed to be my dad, who used to kiss my bumps and scrapes.

Still, I don't respond.

"After all these years, you don't have anything to say to your father?" he prods, his voice laced with curiosity and maybe even a hint of amusement.

I grit my teeth, holding back the anger that threatens to boil over. He abandoned us, leaving my mother and me to fend for ourselves. He has no right to call himself my father.

"You were dead to me the day you walked out on me and my mother," I reply, my voice steady despite the turmoil raging inside me.

Titan's tongue clicks, and I can almost picture him shaking his head. "I'm sure you wish that were true now that you know what really happened to me. I'd say I was sorry, but I don't want to start this conversation out with lies. Though, maybe I underestimated you. You seem to have taken to this life better than I could have predicted all those years ago."

I clench my fists, his words like venom in my veins.

He's trying to get under my skin, to rattle me, but I won't give him the satisfaction.

The sound of wood creaking fills the room, indicating that Titan has moved from his chair. Steady footsteps draw nearer, and I can feel his presence looming over me.

His fingers wrap around my shoulder, and I suppress a shudder of revulsion. "Olivia, I'm still your father, and you're my daughter. It's time for you to act like it and tell me everything you've learned about Luca Monroe."

I bite back a sarcastic retort. He thinks I'm going to help him take down the man whose kept me alive all these weeks? He's out of his goddamn mind. Still, I respond in a different, hopefully safer, way.

"I don't know anything about Luca Monroe other than he's a deranged mafia king who has no qualms about killing people," I say, hoping my resolve comes through my voice.

Titan leans closer, and I can feel his breath on my cheek. "Except you." He steps away, and I can feel his calculating gaze on me. "I thought you were just someone who saw too much and needed to die. Then, I learned Luca was keeping you as his pet. I had hoped by killing you that I could enrage him to the point that he'd make mistakes, but I saw you leave that club. As soon as I knew who you really were, I had other hopes."

I narrow my eyes beneath the blindfold, trying to make sense of his words. What does he mean by "other hopes"? Just that he could use me against Luca?

He moves closer once more, and his voice loses any

semblance of fatherly affection. "Don't disappoint me, Olivia. I know you were fucking him. Tell me what I want to know, and this can be all over."

My heart sinks as I consider just how much Titan already knows. Vin, the traitorous snake who convinced me to leave the safety of Luca's room. He had to have been spying on us this whole time. That fucking bastard.

There's no other way Titan would know my relationship with Luca had become something more. Well, unless there's another defector within Luca's ranks. At least, Titan had the decency to kill Vin. Saves Luca the trouble of doing it himself. Hell, I might have even volunteered to do the murdering once I was out of here. Though, the most important part is that Vin won't be able to go back to Luca, pretending he was tricked and did his best to save me, while continuing to relay important details to Titan.

"Vin would have known more than me," I say with disdain. "What would I know that he didn't *mistakenly* tell you before you murdered him?"

"Vin served his purpose," he responds, thankfully further away from me. "And it was always the plan to kill him. Traitors don't live long in my house, even when they're doing so to better serve me. He only lasted as long as he did because I needed more information about what you were doing with Luca and I was curious about you. The woman I thought you'd become wouldn't have stayed in that house."

I stay silent, refusing to give him the satisfaction of a

reaction. I don't for one second believe this man wanted to know about me because he's worried about my wellbeing or concerned with my choices. Not when he's brought me here tied up.

It sounds as if he sits back down in the chair before speaking again. "Olivia, dear. Please don't fight me. We're family. I'm your father. Don't make me bring your mother into all of this."

Oh, this motherfucker has some nerve. He's also either the biggest idiot in the world or the laziest mafia boss to ever exist.

"Did you only rely on Vin to give you information?" I ask with a sneer, my anger simmering just below the surface. "I'm certain the answer to that question is 'yes,' because if you'd even taken five minutes to do a google search on your *wife*, you'd know she died four weeks ago."

Silence fills the room once more and this time I'm more thankful for it as I fight back tears, digging my nails into my palms. I hope like hell that my mother isn't watching any of this play out. That she's living her best afterlife completely oblivious of the fucked-up world that I've found myself in.

A few minutes later, I hear Titan get up again. Once more, he places a hand on my shoulder, offering what I assume is supposed to be a consoling touch before leaning closer. "I'm sorry. I didn't know. How did she pass?"

The audacity of this man...

I can't take it any longer. I can't pretend that I don't hate him with every fiber of my being and that the feeling doesn't get stronger with every word he speaks.

My head slams toward the sound of his voice, and the side of my face connects somewhere with his, causing him to roar. "You little fucking bitch!"

Titan grabs my hair, holding tight to the bun I'd put it in earlier, and throws me onto the unforgiving floor. With my hands behind my back, I can't cushion the impact. I at least try to turn my body so that I land on my shoulder instead of my face. Still, the impact jolts through me, knocking the breath out of my lungs and making me cry out.

The movements twist me into an awkward position, and my cheek stings from hitting what I believe to be a concrete floor. I start to suck in air, absorbing the pain instead of letting it take control of me, but as soon as I think I can move again, a foot makes a hard connection with my ribs.

"I was going to offer you a place at my side," Titan seethes, spewing what I know is utter bullshit, then kicks me again, this time in my stomach, forcing my body to lurch forward. "But if you'd rather be a whore, protecting someone who's only been using you to get to me, then I'll accept your choice. But if you think Luca didn't know who you were to me, you're sorely mistaken."

He reaches down and grabs the back of my head with one hand while jerking down the blindfold with the other. "Luca knows you're my daughter, Olivia. He only showed you any care as a way to piss me off. You're nothing to him and a senseless little girl if you thought otherwise."

I swallow thickly as I stare into his familiar blue eyes, quickly noticing how deep the lines around his face have become over the years. He doesn't blink or give any other hint that he's lying through his teeth, and I hate even more that I wonder if his harshly spoken words could have any merit.

As much as I believe Luca cares for me now, I'm not naïve enough to pretend that there isn't a chance he chose to only get close to me as a way to enrage his enemy.

Despite the pain, despite the fear, I meet his gaze with defiance. My voice doesn't falter as I speak, my resolve unwavering. "My refusal to do anything you ask has nothing to do with wanting to protect Luca or believing I mean anything to him." I pause, spitting blood out of my mouth and onto the floor. "You did this, *Titan*. You are the reason I look at you and feel nothing. You left us. You're the one that lied. You chose to bring me here as your prisoner and not your daughter. Whatever you think of me or whatever I am to you, it changes nothing."

His grip on my hair tightens, trickles of pain moving from my scalp down my spine, but I manage not to even wince. Not when I know my words have hit their mark. Whatever mind fuck battle he wants to play...I've won this round.

His mouth forms into a hard line as he stares me

down, but I'm not afraid of him. I don't know why. It's not even the same lack of fear I held toward Luca in the beginning.

With Luca, I'd been acting on grief and terror. With Titan, my feelings are built on fury. And if I'm meant to die here, there's nothing I can do about that, but I won't go down without a fight this time. A real fight and not just a calculated one based on wits and emotions.

I'm going to hold on to that hope within the darkness, and I'm going to show my *father* what he really is. A weak fool trying to be someone that he'll never become—a man worth respecting or even fearing.

2

LUCA

Six Hours Earlier

The searing pain in my thigh is nothing compared to the adrenaline pumping through my veins and the overwhelming desire to snuff out the panic within me that can only be doused once I've returned to the apartment, ensuring Olivia's safety. Though, I know I can't ignore the bullet wound forever.

Blood drips behind me as I hobble into the elevator, my fingers trembling as I press the button for the fourth floor. Damon joins me just before the doors close, eyeing me with concern.

"You look like shit," he states with little emotion in his tone. "You're lucky the bullet went straight through."

"And you're a dick," I retort, then glance down. "How do you know?"

He points to the front and back of my thigh. "You're bleeding from both sides. You'd know that if you took two seconds to take care of yourself."

"I only care that all those fuckers are dead and then getting back to Olivia." I refuse to stop until I put eyes on her. She has to be scared shitless after hearing the mayhem from up there.

His lips tighten into a flat line. "Not all of them are dead."

He's right. There's one man that we didn't find, the one responsible for putting a target on my back—Titan Moretti. His increased bounty on Olivia drew enemies like vultures, leading to the attack on my home that we've only just barely survived.

The elevator stops and the doors part, but before I've even taken a step, all the blood rushes from my head and I have to grip the bar next to me before I pass out.

"That door is never open, Damon," I say through gritted teeth. That means someone has been up here who shouldn't have been, and I will fucking kill whoever it was.

There's a hidden panel in the wall on my floor, one that leads to a stairwell and exits out into the garage. It's something very few people have known about over the years.

Damon is already moving, gun out and surveying the area. "Your apartment door is open."

"Fuck," I snarl, thrusting myself forward and ignoring the stabbing pain that shoots up through my body.

And the door isn't charred from the electrical security I activated before leaving, meaning someone entered with the code.

The only people who have that are Jaxon, Damon, Markus, and Vin. I know for damn sure it wasn't Jaxon or Damon, but Markus or Vin? Who the fuck knows, but I'm going to find out.

Walking into the living room of my apartment, there aren't any signs of a struggle, and I don't hear Olivia, but still, I call out her name as my heart races.

The resounding silence has my fists tightening and jaw clenching as I struggle to breathe through the rage and pain circulating inside my body. Not only that but the fear. It's been years since I've had a reason to be afraid. Though, I'm not afraid for myself. It's the rest of the world that needs to be scared if I don't find Olivia soon.

With regret and utter disgust at myself for having left her unprotected, I say, "She's not here. We need to check the stairs."

"You can't go down them like that," Damon says, nodding at my leg. "I'm going to go ahead and see if I find anything. You take the elevator. Jaxon will meet you down there to help you across the garage."

My chest sucks air in harshly before delivering a rough exhale that burns through my lungs with the intensity of my ire. I want to argue, but I know better.

Damon's right, and Olivia's life is on the line. The

longer we stand here, the less likely we are to find her, which is fucking unacceptable to me.

With a curt nod, I move toward the elevator and catch Damon lift his phone to his ear before racing down the stairs.

Once I'm moving south, I reach for the pistol in my waistband and check the mag, making sure that if there are people who still need to be killed that I can be the one to provide that service. I need every motherfucker's head on a spike to even stand a chance of quelching the fury storming through me.

I double-check the bandage around my thigh. It's soaked with crimson all the way around but holding tight. Though, even looking down makes me dizzy, so I know I've lost more than enough blood. Still, the wound will have to wait.

Exiting the elevator, Jaxon is standing there and holds his arms out. "Want me to carry you?"

"I will put a bullet in your head if you so much as touch me," I growl, my worry for Olivia making me even more irritable.

"Too soon for jokes, got it," he titters. "But I do need to touch you or it's going to take you too long to hobble your crippled ass over to the other side of the garage."

He's not wrong, so with reluctance, I lift my arm and position it over his shoulders as he holds tight around my waist, taking a lot of the weight off my leg. I hate to admit that helps, but we're moving and almost running within seconds, so I have no problem giving him my muttered thanks once we get to where Damon is standing over a body.

"Vin is dead," he announces. "Not sure if that's because he was trying to save your girl or if he was the reason she's no longer in her room."

Seeing his body without a weapon drawn confirms what I knew the moment the elevator opened to my floor. We had a traitor within our ranks this whole time and I don't even get the pleasure of torturing him myself. That thought serves to further enrage me.

I should have seen this coming. I should have done more to protect what's mine.

"What about the video feed?" Jaxon asks, and I nearly strangle myself at not having thought of that the moment I saw the panel door open upstairs.

How could I have not thought to check the cameras? Not that I need any further confirmation of Vin's betrayal, but I need to have eyes on Olivia. To see that she was at least unharmed when she was taken.

Damon is already doing so on his phone, and I move closer to see the screen myself. Sure enough, there is Vin at my door, punching in the code as if he lives there himself.

"Turn the volume up," I say, wanting to hear how this went down.

Olivia is a smart woman. She wouldn't have just gone along with things for the sake of doing so.

I listen intently as Vin plays her, spewing lies and half-truths from his mouth. Though, there is a sense of pride as I watch my Raven keep a gun that I didn't give her pointed at him and question the fuck out of him.

Unfortunately, I don't blame her for going with him by the end of the conversation. He had the code. She knows I trusted him. He allowed her to remain armed. She had no reason to distrust him.

Once they head down the stairs, Damon turns the screen off, then begins digging through Vin's pockets, pulling out his cell phone, unlocking it with a code Damon shouldn't know. Though, it doesn't surprise me in the least that he does.

I watch as he goes through his text messages and tense when he growls. "Vin has been working against us for months. Titan was blowing his ego up, promising that Vin would be running this compound within six months, and in Titan's words, just like he should have been doing since your father's death."

Fuck. It isn't as if I've spent years keeping Vin at arm's length. He's been given important tasks and trusted without hesitation. Though, I can't deny there have been moments when I've known he's wanted more from me, and I haven't allowed him in.

"Find them and get her back, Damon," I seethe. "Do it fucking now. And if you don't, I'll start killing people every hour until I find her myself."

I'm growing weaker by the second, but as soon as I'm stitched up, the scum that live in this city better hide, because it's not just Titan I'm coming for. I'll hunt every son of a bitch who even considered cashing in on that bounty and taking Olivia from me.

I won't stop until the streets run with red and I have her back safe and sound. And if she's not returned to me...

The world will know the consequences of Titan's mistake when he decided to fuck with me.

3

OLIVIA

The night stretches on, and Titan remains absent. My hands are still bound behind my back as I lean against the wall, but at least the blindfold is now resting against my neck, giving me some limited view of the room. I search for a place to lie down, hoping to find some rest amidst this nightmare.

Through the barred and tinted window, I catch glimpses of the setting sun, leaving me wondering about Luca and his safety. Vin had mentioned Luca being shot. Was it a lie? Could he have used that as an excuse for not rescuing me personally? Should I even care?

If Titan is right and Luca was only using me to get to him, there's a chance he's not even looking for me. He made no promises of affection, only that he would keep me safe. Now that he's failed at that...

I give my head a solid shake. I can't go there right

now. It's a worry for future me and not an added stress that I need right now.

Surveying the rest of the room, I realize there's no comfortable place to sleep. No couch, no padded chair, only a wooden table and hard seats. Next to that stands a locked metal cabinet, tempting me with thoughts of breaking it open if only I had access to my hands.

Still resting against the wall, I close my eyes and take a deep breath. The events of the day have left me exhausted, but my will to survive and escape Titan remains resolute. He may physically break me, but not mentally. I'll fight until my dying breath to regain my freedom, because he doesn't deserve to have this win over me. I'm more sure of that than anything else right now.

An itch irritates my nose, and I groan in frustration. My face has never itched so much in my life, taunting me further with my inability to use my hands properly. Worse, I desperately need to use the bathroom and can't undo my jeans in this condition.

As I contemplate knocking myself out to avoid the humiliation of wetting myself, I come up with a better idea. One I should have thought of hours ago. Maybe I can merely slip my arms out from under me, forcing them to stretch past my feet. Movies make it seem so easy.

Knowing that I'm not the most limber or agile person in the world, I lower myself to the ground, then push my ass out as far as I can contort my body. The cotton rope tying my wrists together gets stuck on the back of my pants, but I jerk hard and then wince loudly from the strain on my shoulders.

Oh, I'm totally fucked now.

With my hands pressed firmly beneath my ass and my arms feeling as if they're going to be pulled out of their sockets, I lay my head on the ground and close my eyes again, trying to calm the panic clawing its way up my throat.

I can do this. I just need to relax and trust that my body is capable of being as flexible as I need it to be. I've done yoga. Once. This is totally fine.

It's not as if my ribs aren't also screaming at me thanks to the beating Titan decided to give me earlier. The pain is nothing if not motivation to get free.

Another deep breath and I feel the muscles in my battered body finally begin to do as I've pleaded, the discomfort slowly fading away. With another swift tug, I pull my arms further down while bending myself inward as much as possible.

One foot slips through above my wrists, and I nearly pause due to the awkwardness of this position—it's definitely not as easy as the movies make it look—but I know if I stop, I'm going to be in an even more difficult position than just a few moments ago.

I force myself to push through the agony and am pretty sure I hear a pop in my ankle as I do, but when I'm laid out on the floor, chest heaving and body free to lay how it naturally wants to...nothing hurts as if it's broken. Just severely unhappy about my current predicament.

I'm about to sleep on a concrete floor tonight. My body better get over it, because I need to be at my best tomorrow when I assume Titan will return.

After a short reprieve, I give myself another onceover, running my hands over my legs and pressing in areas to test my injuries. Unfortunately, I can't seem to get the restraints off my hands, but at least I can defend myself better with them in front of me.

The dim light flickers above me, and I hope they're going to turn it off, but minutes tick by with no such luck. I can at least admit this is better than being kept in complete darkness at all times, like before.

Forcing myself to stand again, I make my way toward the only door I can see in this room. Since there isn't a bucket, finding a spot on the floor is my only other option if I'm to relieve myself. And better on the floor than in my pants.

I shove my jeans down, one push at a time, and use the wall to help keep me balanced since my wrists are still bound together. As soon as I stick my ass far enough away from my pants, I take care of business, ignoring the tiny splatters that bounce back up and remind me that I could have peed myself instead. Plus, this way, hopefully Titan will step in the puddle, making my day.

Once I'm done, I know it's time to get some rest and head toward the furthest corner in the room. Uncomfortably so, I inch my way down to the floor and choose to try and sleep sitting up. My body might hate me a little less in the morning. Probably not, but the position at least seems more comfortable than when I was lying flat on the floor a few minutes ago.

I close my eyes and picture the garden in Luca's private courtyard. Had it only been hours ago that I was there, losing myself to my art and allowing myself to believe that being with Luca wouldn't be the end of the world?

Thinking of that moment has me unable to block out my earlier questions about whether or not Luca is searching for me. I want to believe that I'm not that big of a fool to have fallen for him without him returning the sentiment.

Those moments when he held me... couldn't have all been fake.

If they were, I'll find a way to move past it just as soon as I get the hell out of this place. I won't let the "what if" questions drive me to the point of insanity, not when I need to keep my fury focused on Titan.

I settle in for a long night on a cold floor, but before my breathing can even out, I hear the door open. My head turns to see who has entered the room, but before I can get a look at the new arrival, the lights are turned off, plunging the room into darkness.

My body tenses up as I listen intently to the sounds of the footfalls. Ones so soft that I'm not sure if they completely miss the mess I just made or are just that light. Whoever is there comes closer, but there is no sense of urgency in the movements I hear. Why should there be? I'm a captive, tied up with nothing to defend myself with.

Except I'm not in the same position I was with Titan earlier. I have my strength and the innate will to live. With that knowledge, I take a steadying breath and wait for whoever has joined me to make his first move.

There's a small possibility that nothing will happen, but that's just wishful thinking. In the next second, rough hands grab on to my hair and slam my head against the drywall behind me.

I suck in a breath and begin to panic, but then remind myself that I'm not helpless. I might not have had very much time in the gym with Justine, but she showed me I'm stronger than I've ever given myself credit for. More than that, I told myself earlier that I wasn't going down without a fight. I'm going to keep that promise.

Gathering my bearings, I punch forward with both hands still tied together, aiming for a dick or even a kidney, but it's hard to tell where anything is in the darkness. Instead of either of my marks, I miss and hit air.

A deep grumbly voice chuckles. "Nice try, little girl."

He pulls me by my hair again, and I move my legs quickly to take the strain off my scalp. As soon as I'm on two feet, I thrust my knee forward. This time I don't miss. His balls get crunched and hopefully a few things broken, but the win is swiftly dashed away.

My attacker slams his fist into the side of my head, forcing my skull to bounce off the wall and back into his waiting palm that then slaps me across the cheek, all of which explodes with pain that I can't manage to ignore. Though, I'm glad the walls are covered in drywall and not concrete like the floor.

Mother fuck fuck.

A finger drags over my cheek, taking my blood with it, and it takes everything in me to stay conscious as I grip his wrists, begging my body to fight back, but not knowing where to find the strength.

"Daddy Dearest said I wasn't allowed to kill you, but he suggested I teach you a lesson or two about loyalty." His whispered words send a chill down my spine.

"He might be *your* daddy, but Titan is nothing to me," I say with venom that only serves to make him laugh again.

"I was hoping you'd say that." His fingers wrap around my neck, squeezing as he starts to lift my body from the ground.

The air in my lungs leaves quicker than I wish, raising my panic, and the likelihood that I'll be awake much longer isn't high. Except I can't stand the thought of this man *teaching* lessons while I'm not conscious to fight back.

I force my arms to rise, knowing he's right in front of me thanks to his hold on me, and lightly feel for his face, acting only slightly weaker than I really am. His cheeks are clean shaven, but I don't bother to suss out any other details. I find his eyes and then use the last of my resolve to shove my thumbs into his eye sockets. A feat easier to do than I would have thought, as long as I ignore the squishy, wet feeling as I press harder.

He'll have to choose between letting go of me or risk going blind in at least one eye. At this point, I don't really care which happens. Either way, I'll win. Even if it's only in a small way.

"You fucking bitch," he snarls, and I grin into the darkness.

He releases my neck, and I drop to the ground in a heap, landing on my elbows and saving my head from another injury.

I sense the attacker coming closer and feel his hot breath on my face as he bends down to taunt me, whispering, "I was told you were a fighter, Raven. Good to see it's true."

Everything inside my body turns to ice. *Raven.* Is he calling me that because he knows Luca or because Vin shared that information and the name is meant to fuck with my mind?

Hope or despair? It could be either one, and I have no clue how to know which is the truth.

He stands and kicks me in the thigh hard enough to have my body instinctively curling in on itself to protect my midsection. Bruising and broken bones I can heal from, but internal bleeding might be a bit much if I don't get out of here soon enough.

His departure isn't quiet as his feet stomp across the room, and I get one last smirk when I hear the sound of a splash once he's at the door.

He snarls, but mercifully, doesn't return to retaliate. I listen as the door opens, then slams closed. I expect the lights to come back on to add to my suffering, but I'm left in the darkness. A small blessing in the shit storm of beatings.

I stay curled in a ball on the floor, slowing my breathing and trying to determine if there are any injuries I need to be concerned with before I allow my body to finally pass out. My hand lightly touches my face and head. There's blood on my scalp, but not enough that I need to bother with trying to cover it with a strip of my shirt.

A lump protrudes from the side of my head where my skull became acquainted with the guy's fist and the wall, but it's just swollen and not another open wound. It hurts to swallow after being choked, but again, not something I need to worry about now.

With that knowledge, I allow myself to drift off into the darkness. Rest is my only friend until I'm free. I'll need as much of it as I can get, because I suspect this first beating is just one of many to come my way unless I give in, which I won't.

They'll be relentless unless I agree to work with Titan. A fleeting thought crosses my mind that I should just give in. Agree to work with him and tell him what little I do know to save my own hide, but just as quickly as the thought comes, it's dashed away.

Luca hasn't been in my life long, but he's cared for me in his own way. He's done his best to protect me, paid for all of my debts, made me that garden where I could paint, and he ignites a fire within my body that nobody else has ever come close to matching.

No, I won't turn on him. Not even to save my own life. I'm a better person than that, with more honor than any of these men. On top of that, even though it might be stupid after what Titan said, I'm still holding out hope that Luca meant what he said before. That if anything happened to me, he'd burn the city to find me.

With that final glimmer of hope, I surrender to sleep, praying for a better tomorrow.

4

LUCA

Blood drips from my chin, an untamed river of vengeance marking my progress through the chaos I've orchestrated. The air resonates with the metallic tang of blood, mingling with the stench of sweat and desperation. I stand over one of the many bodies I've slain in the last hour, each fallen form serving as testament to the wrath that consumes me.

Each and every one of them has been useless to me, mere pawns in the twisted game they've found themselves caught in. Unless I give them credit for allowing me to take my...aggressions out on them.

Though, it's not as if they were willing to die. Their pathetic attempts at fighting back or pleading with me revealed their fragility. Their cries, begging for their lives, all fall on deaf ears.

I wipe the blade of my knife over my black jeans, the fabric absorbing the crimson evidence of my wrath. I spit on the dead body at my feet, a final display of contempt for another gang being useless in helping me get Olivia back. "Fucking scum."

Jaxon leans against the grimy brick wall of the alleyway, his posture relaxed, arms crossed in an almost casual stance. He watches as if I'm grocery shopping and not slitting throats. "You'll be making headlines before you know it at this rate," he muses, his voice a curious blend of admiration and mockery.

I ignore his remark, the echo of his words blending with the adrenaline thudding in my veins as I soak up the cool night air. The bodies might make headlines, but there will never be a link to me or my crew. Damon makes sure of that each and every time. I don't always know how, but he's never let me down and I'm certain he won't this time, either.

I walk toward the waiting SUV, its sleek black exterior providing a stark contrast to the sordid scene I'm leaving behind. Damon sits in the driver's seat, his hands resting calmly on the steering wheel, a sentinel guarding the entrance to the alleyway while I've had my fun.

Olivia has been missing for three nights now. Three interminable nights that have wrapped around me like a vice, suffocating my every thought. There have been no demands from Titan, no threats, no nothing. Jaxon and Damon have tried to convince me that's a good thing, but I don't see how no news in this instance could be considered anything other than a mindfuck.

Not knowing if she's already dead is driving me mad,

and just as I promised, the streets are running red, along with several buildings having already burned because of it, dozens of people killed in my search for Olivia.

Every corner, every shadow, they all whisper her name to me. But I'm yet to hear her voice, and that thought gnaws at my sanity a little more with each passing hour.

I open the back door of the SUV, but Damon throws a towel at me with a faint smirk playing on his lips. "Murders aside, we're not savages," he states matter-of-factly. "Clean yourself up."

He's right. I'm normally not this...eccentric with my work. Taking men back to the compound is my typical style, but I don't have time to go through them one-by-one. I need answers now. I wipe the towel across my face, removing the traces of death that cling to me. It's a futile attempt to cleanse myself, but at least my appearance is less grim now.

Once I've soaked up the excess blood, I get into the back seat. Jaxon is already in the front, but he reaches back to hand me a syringe, a lifeline that's becoming more frequent. "Time to juice up unless you're done for the night."

It's been hours since I've thought of my bullet wound. The pain that was a constant companion is now a dull throb, buried beneath layers of medications and determination. I push away the syringe filled with some sort of cocktail drug, resisting the urge to become dependent on its false energy. "I don't need it."

Jaxon raises an eyebrow, a silent challenge in his gaze. "You say that now, but in an hour, when the last dose wears off and you realize the damage that you're doing by not fucking resting, you're going to wish you'd taken this."

I glare at him, his words a frustrating truth that I want to deny. But I know he's right. I can't continue like this. I sigh in reluctant concession. "Just give it to me," I grumble.

I fucking hate medication. Even more so that I'm dependent on this boost to keep me going, but I can't stop until I get Olivia back.

She deserves at least this much from me. If I'd just let her go that day at the hotel... If I hadn't let my selfish desires cloud my judgment... She wouldn't be in this nightmare. It's a guilt that eats away at me, and it's foreign to my emotions.

But I couldn't ignore the draw to her, nor the soul-deep innocence and light that radiated from her even when she was terrified. I needed that in my life more than I needed my next breath. And I still do.

The only saving grace is that those closest to me have understood. Jaxon, Damon, and even Markus, who prefers to keep to the shadows, haven't slept for long since my Raven was taken, helping me with anything I demand of them.

Our home is in shambles, but Justine has been put in charge of repairs and delegating those I approve of to mend the broken windows, shattered walls, and other reminders of the siege the compound endured. Most importantly, a new security system has been put in place. I paid triple the amount and had it done yesterday. I need to know that when I bring Olivia home she's going to be safe. Any other outcome is unacceptable.

While she should have been fine in my apartment with the steel shutters and electricity-filled door, she wasn't. I want to make sure that nobody can ever get into the house again to put us in the same position.

"Back to Roe, or toward the north side of the city?" Damon asks as I jab the needle into my thigh, the sensation more familiar than I care to admit.

"Considering I just stabbed myself so I can keep going," I reply with a wry smile, trying to ignore the racing of my heart and the slight difficulty in breathing while the cocktail of pharmaceuticals works its way through me. "North side of town, and then we can call it a night."

It's nearing two in the morning. I've at least tried to have them back to the house by sunrise these last two days, only for us to head out a few hours later.

Jaxon holds his phone, his fingers dancing over the screen as he speaks. "The next group is called Blood Runners."

Seriously? What is wrong with people? That's a terrible fucking name unless they literally run blood, which is highly unlikely.

"There are at least a dozen in the crew," Jaxon continues, reading from his phone. "Raymond is the leader, and he's been in the game of hookers and drugs for the last ten years, taking over for his uncle named...Craig Ventelli."

Ventelli... The name sounds familiar, but I can't place him. Maybe someone my father did business with? Wouldn't surprise me. Even though he tried to hide his darker dealings from me, I've never been oblivious to those around me.

Well, except for Vin. Though, that wasn't so much obliviousness. It was overconfidence. I didn't think there was a chance in hell that a member of my team who had been around as long as Vin would turn against me.

It's a mistake I don't intend to repeat.

Jaxon continues to go on about the warehouse they do their business in and the number of women they might have there, along with the various kinds of drugs that they dabble in—cocaine being their bread and butter.

I've never understood how someone could thrive making money on a product likely to ruin the lives of not only the person buying, but anyone else around them. I might not have qualms about murder that's almost always deserved, but drugs disgust me. Needlessly taking lives with a substance that can't often be controlled, or worse, likely using the addictive drug to control the women they whore out... The thought makes me eager to get to this warehouse and teach these lowlifes a lesson or two.

By the time we arrive at our destination, my heart rate has slowed to a manageable level, and I've reloaded each of my mags before double checking that my go-to knife is tucked securely in its sheath behind my back.

The warehouse, as we approach, is a desolate structure, its decrepit appearance a metaphor for the corrupted souls dwelling within. Gripping my weapons, I step out of the SUV, flanked by the unwavering support of Damon and Jaxon. The night air is a frigid embrace, a stark contrast to the intensity burning within me.

My foot slams against the rusted door, the metallic clang resonating in the stillness. A twinge of pain courses through my body, a reminder of the wound I carry. Yet, the influx of adrenaline, a companion familiar and intoxicating, surges through me, subduing the ache.

The frame of the door is compromised, and we push through it, knocking the busted lock to the ground as we do. It's not as if anyone will be able to use this building by the time we've finished our business here.

The inside is cast in a murky illumination, emanating from hanging overhead lights. The air hangs heavy with the musty scent of decay, as if the building itself has already thrown in the towel on its own existence.

The tables beneath the lights are topped with computers and papers, surrounded by chairs that only a handful of men fill. Behind them are partitioned spaces constructed from plywood and curtains and shrouded in darkness where I assume they sort their drugs or make their women work.

A group of five men start to scatter, but the building is too sparse to hide quickly enough. Bullets start to fly before they can duck or even pull out their own guns.

Three go down within seconds, and the other two

stand frozen with their hands up. "Hey, man. We just work here. Take whatever you want."

His smoker's voice instantly grates on my last nerve, and I put a bullet through the center of his forehead before turning my attention to the remaining man.

He shakes where he stands but doesn't make a move or speak as I stalk closer, pistol still drawn. "How many more are here?"

Dark blue eyes meet mine, and he speaks with assurance. "Sixteen women, four visitors, and another eight men upstairs that are probably on their way down here right now."

His confidence allows a flicker of hope to sputter inside my chest that maybe this will be where I find answers that lead me closer to Olivia.

Damon and Jaxon are already moving toward where the other eight men might be hiding. I wait patiently, keeping the barrel of my gun pressed into the man's chest in front of me.

He has a buzzed head, no scars or even tattoos. Not the normal type I find in these situations, but I'm not here to judge. At least, not in that way.

More gunshots echo through the buildings, screams rip through the air, and doors slam, but I stay unmoving, as does the man in front of me.

I take in his plain black tee, cheap jeans, and dirty white sneakers before appraising his round face once more. "What's your name?"

"Simon."

I scoff. Why does that feel so fitting for him?

"Well, Simon." I press the gun a little harder to his chest. "Why don't you start talking while my friends get acquainted with yours?"

His face pales as he speaks. "I only manage the books. I don't know anything about what they do here."

A sardonic smile tugs at my lips, an embodiment of my incredulity. "Oh, Simon. You damn well know what they do here. The fact that you still show up every day to do your job is reason enough to kill you."

He spits and sputters, trying to talk over his fear. "I don't have a choice."

The end of my pistol taps over his cheek. "We always have a choice."

Women start to run toward us, but I stop them with a glare. "Don't leave this building."

I don't bother to threaten them with words as the six naked whores all halt in their tracks. My tone and the gun in my hand is enough. If they're here, they've been conditioned enough to know when to listen, so I use that to my advantage.

The last thing we need is anyone calling for help or making a scene and ruining my fun.

Simon takes a step back, but I close the distance. "You're not going anywhere, and if you move again, it will be the last thing you ever do."

He swallows hard but doesn't even attempt to nod. At least he's not a complete idiot.

"Does your boss Raymond ever do business with

Titan Moretti?" I ask him as I continue to wait for Jaxon and Damon to return.

Sweat drops down Simon's temples. "I'd need to look the name up on my computer."

My gun taps his head again. "Then, let's go."

As he begins to walk with my permission, I glance back at the women, uninterested in their naked bodies, but needing them to know I haven't forgotten, nor will I forget, about their presence here. "If you stay right where you are and remain quiet, you can take every dollar stashed in this place when we're done here."

One black-haired beauty that momentarily reminds me of Olivia steps forward, chin tilted up. "Why should we believe that you're not just like them and don't intend to take us?"

"You shouldn't," I say confidently. "Do better for yourselves. But stay the fuck out of my way before you do."

Two of the other women tug on her wrists, pulling her back to the group, and I dismiss them. I don't have time to placate anyone. I need to find Titan and rip his head from his shoulders or maybe even bash his skull in with my fists. I've even envisioned cutting him over and over again until he bleeds to death, strapped to a table.

Simon is typing at the computer, and I force away the darker thoughts to watch every key he presses, making sure he's not somehow alerting anyone of our arrival at the warehouse. When he types in Moretti's name, I tense, waiting for what I need to show up on the screen.

The name I seek materializes on the screen, the revelation both gratifying and maddening. My grip tightens on Simon's shoulder, a silent affirmation of my expectations. "Click on it."

With a shaky hand, he does as I've commanded, and I scan the available information there. Most of it I already have, like the address to the house where we blew up the kitchen, his name and phone number, and even date of birth.

Just when I'm about to shoot this bumbling idiot in the head for being useless, he opens another window. "I'm not sure what you're looking for, but here's his banking information from a past transfer we completed with him."

I personally can't do anything with the account numbers, but Jaxon might be able to. He enjoys working with his FBI guy on some stuff. Maybe he'll come through with a different address linked to the account for us to check out.

I take a picture of the screen with my phone and raise my gun in the air. My intent is only to knock him out, but when a woman screams from behind me, I hesitate.

"Don't hurt him," she pleads, covering her fake tits with one arm and the pussy I have no interest in with the other. "He's only here because of me."

"And who are you?" I ask, not that I should care, but she's risking my wrath for his life. Call me intrigued since he was possibly helpful.

Her eyes cast toward him, almost apologetically. "I'm

his wife. I had a drug problem and got myself into some trouble with Raymond. This is how we're paying him back."

Fucking Olivia. I blame the fact that she made me care for her so damn much for my next words.

"Fine," I say with regret and hope that doesn't bite me in the ass later. "But if I ever see either of you again in a setting that is anything close to this, I will kill you both without thinking twice."

"We'll be out of this state by sunrise," she promises, running toward Simon. I move away from them, because their love only serves to fuel my fury.

I need Olivia back. Right the fuck now.

Damon and Jaxon reappear, a man being dragged by the former. His face is swollen, and blood is dripping from somewhere on his body, but he's still conscious.

Damon throws him on the ground at my feet. "This is Raymond."

The tension around me rises exponentially from the waiting women as their murmurs start up.

I grab him by the collar of his black dress shirt and lift him with one hand until he's on his knees, then force his head to turn toward the whores. "You ruined their lives, but I'm going to give them a chance to fix that."

My gun points at the group as I say my next words. "My earlier threat applies to all of you. If I see any of you involved in any of the darker shit you've seen here, I will kill you. No warning, no excuses, just death." The pistol moves back to Raymond, and without blinking, I pull the trigger.

He falls back to the floor, and I glance at the women one last time. "Consider that bullet your ticket to freedom. Grab whatever you want from this place within the next five minutes. After that, it'll be on fire."

None of them hesitate. They all scatter toward the back of the building. Well, all of them expect Simon and his...wife.

Jaxon grins. "That was, uh, nice of you."

I ignore his comment. "Did you learn anything?"

He shakes his head. "But we flushed all the drugs and killed each of his men, so the world is a little better off."

The fuck it is. Not with Olivia still missing.

I text Jaxon the picture I took. "Get me an address to that account number. It's one of Titan's." Then, I nod at Damon, holding my hand out. "Keys. I'm going to wait in the car. Even if those women aren't done, burn this cesspool in four minutes."

As I turn around, I see Simon's back already moving out the door. They didn't even bother to try to steal what they likely deserved. Good for them. At least that's what I think, until I realize he was the accountant. He probably had funds transferred to an offshore account the moment I pulled the trigger. If so, I'd be slightly impressed, but I don't care enough to find out.

I get to the SUV, unlock it, and slide into the back, this time laying down to get as much pressure off my leg as possible.

I'm a fucking wreck in more ways than one, but I won't give up. Olivia is mine, and I'm going to have her again. Titan may be more resourceful than I originally gave him credit for, but my motivation is never-ending.

There won't be a sewer he can hide in that will stop me from eventually finding him and ending his sorry excuse for a life.

5

OLIVIA

The world around me is a swirl of pain and darkness. My swollen face distorts my vision, and every inch of my body throbs with agony. Sleeping on the cold, unforgiving floor has left me with aches that are more than just physical–they are the echoes of the beatings I've endured. Though, it's not as if I've been sleeping, more like slipping in and out of consciousness from the sheer pain.

Titan, the man I used to think of as a father, has only returned once during these endless hours or days. Time has lost all meaning in this room. When he did visit, his presence was a menacing shadow, his gaze filled with disdain as he stared down at me, shook his head, and called me a disappointment.

Like, what in the actual fuck?

I used to pray for his return as a young girl, clinging to the image of the man my mother loved. Her unwavering devotion to him made me believe that he was a good person who had lost his way. But reality is a brutal teacher. I have no clue if my mother hid his darker side from me or was somehow oblivious to it. I'll likely never know.

Though the longer I'm here, the more certain I am that Titan isn't just a man who lost his temper; he's a sadistic monster who must have manipulated my mother. I hope she can't see him now, because I think she'd die all over again, which is a thought I can't handle right now.

The door creaks open again, and I don't bother to lift my head or move from my huddled position on the floor. Each beating has chipped away at my inner strength, making it hard to draw on the relentlessness I had about escaping. My spirit feels shattered, my will to fight back worn down by the brutality. The more I fight back, the less energy I have to stay awake.

Even with a rotation of men that attempt to beat me into submission, there's a part of me that still hasn't given up all hope. I can't die in this place. I refuse to believe that this is my destiny. I haven't been through everything I have in the last month for my life to end like this.

I might not have a fairytale in my future, but I'm going to find happiness if it's the last thing I do.

One saving grace is that not all of the attackers have been as brutal as I expected. I can rarely tell who is who, but one hits just a little less than the rest, and none of them have commented about my thumbs trying to blind them that first night. Nor have they used the name Raven.

At this point, I half wonder if I imagined it, but I'll never really know.

The lights dim again, and the stomp of heavy feet comes my way. When they stop, I tense, expecting a boot to greet my ribs as it so often has lately, but the hit doesn't come. I try to see who's there, but between my swollen eyes and the lack of light, all I see are shadows.

Though, I don't miss it when the man bends closer, shoves a piece of plastic into my palm, then whispers, "Are you ready to fight, Raven?"

The breath catches in my throat. Is this the same man from the first night? The one I'd just been wondering if I imagined? It has to be. None of the others have used that nickname. Yet, my hackles are still up, because only Luca has ever called me that and I need to know who this stranger is.

I try to get a better look at him, but he grabs me by the back of my neck, turning my body as he lifts it. "You're going to use that shiv to stab me and then you're going to run. Do you understand?"

"Run where?" I match his whispered tone, holding the plastic tighter as my heart begins to race, fueling the adrenaline I'm going to need to force my body to move in ways it's not going to want to.

He shoves me forward, and I nearly end up stabbing myself as I'm thrown against the wall. Though, my body isn't jarred as much as I would have expected before he handed me a weapon.

His grip on my hair guides my head until his face is close to mine. I still can't see his features clearly, but I can feel his intensity. When there's a tug at my pants, panic surges within me, but he stops whatever he was doing before I can react fully. "Out the door, turn left, go up the stairs right in front of you. Once you're at that door, go right and don't stop running, Olivia. This is the only chance you're going to get. Nobody is coming for you."

My heart hammers in my chest, and my skin tingles. Fuck. I can hardly breathe and I'm in danger of passing out, but I force myself to calm down. I have no clue if I can trust this guy, but I haven't had any other options in however long I've been here, and his use of "Raven" gives me the slightest hope that he knows Luca.

But then again...if he knew Luca, why didn't he tell him where I was? Why wouldn't anyone be coming for me?

Damn it. If I make another wrong choice like I did with Vin... I can't.

My potential savior squeezes his fingers around my biceps and snarls. "Are you fucking listening to me? One chance. That's all you have. Tomorrow you die. Now, fight back unless death is what you've been wishing for."

I'm out of time. I have to make a choice, and I choose to live. To keep fighting.

He moves me in front of his body and grabs the front of my neck. His chest and stomach are completely exposed, and the weapon in my hand grows heavy as I consider where to stab him.

If he's truly helping me, I don't want to kill him. Then again, he's beaten on me at least once and he chooses to stay here with Titan. Maybe the world would be better off without him.

I nearly snort. I've been spending too much time with the mafia.

His grip gets tighter, and my throat burns. With one glance behind him, I see the door to my cage has been left open and decide to take a leap of faith.

I'm getting the hell out of here.

My arm moves forward as hard and fast as I'm currently capable of. The tip of the plastic shiv cuts into his side, and I swear he twists inward to hurt himself further.

"Go," he snarls, grasping at my wrists, but not really holding on.

I don't hesitate this time. I repeat his earlier instructions. Left at the door, up the stairs, then right and run. That's all I have to do. I just need to run.

My legs move, but every time my feet connect with the floor, a shock of pain shoots through my body and tears threaten to spill from the agony. Still, I don't stop, focusing on getting to safety and praying that I can muster enough adrenaline to even make it past the stairs.

I yank the door the rest of the way open, dodge left, and see the stairwell. The thought of climbing them already has me wanting to give up, but I refuse. They'll have to shoot me in the back before I quit. I grip the railing and force my body to keep going. To ignore the raging anguish coursing through me and to keep fighting just a little longer.

All I have to do is make it out of this place, get help, and find Luca. Nothing more and nothing less.

An alarm starts to blare as I reach the top of the stairs, making me freeze for seconds that I know I don't have.

I hear shouts, but with the pounding in my head, I can't tell where they're coming from. Instead, I brave whatever I'm about to find beyond this door and pull it open.

My eyes burn from the bright light. I can't tell where I am, but I go right, listening to the stranger's instructions. The shouts get louder, but I don't stop moving my legs, even if they are getting slower.

There's another door. A big one. I squint, doing my best to focus amongst the shrieking sounds around me, and turn my head until I figure out where the hell I am.

It's a house. Like a normal house with photos I can't focus on hung on the walls and a living room with couches and a table and shit on it.

I don't have time to be surprised. All I can do is keep moving forward. My hand grips the door handle, and it mercifully opens.

"She's at the front door," a man yells from behind me.

Mother fuck fuck.

The door is thrown open, and I hobble my sorry ass through the threshold. I'm in a residential area, and it's dark. Too dark. None of the houses have lights on, and I won't get someone to open the door before one of these psychos drags my ass back to what I now assume is a basement.

Knowing my time is short, I reach back and close the door behind me to hide my next move and hope it's not too simple that I'm about to get caught, but just simple enough that nobody will realize what I've done.

Next to the front porch are massive hydrangea bushes. It's the only spot I can get to quickly enough in my condition and that's exactly what I do. I throw myself into the plant and curl into the smallest ball I can form as I work to slow my breathing and remain silent.

The door opens and feet stomp on the wood slats very close to my head. "She's half-dead," Titan's voice snarls. "She can't have gotten that far. Go fucking finish her."

I blink back tears that I want to say are only because of the pain that swirls through me as I force myself to stay as small as possible. It shouldn't hurt that my father wants me dead. Not after what I've seen and learned. But no matter what I've said...that monster was once my dad.

There had been a brief moment when I saw him in that SUV that I thought I might get one of my parents back. I'd let the happy memories of my childhood resurface until this man showed me who he really is.

A psychopath. A pathetic excuse of a human being.

Still, he was my father until I was nine years old, before he disappeared, running away from a gambling debt—at least that was the story I'd been told. The man who taught me how to ride a bike, who let me stand on his shiny black shoes at our first daddy-daughter dance because I was too nervous to move on my own, and who tucked me into the tightest burrito every night before bed until I got "too cool" for that.

My chest feels as if it's being ripped open as I grieve a parent I lost long ago. Not only that, but for my mother, who waited on him to return to her, who believed in the man he somehow convinced her he was.

The front door slams, but I can't tell if I'm alone. Tears fall down my cheeks, my face in the cool dirt with leaves and branches from the bush covering my body. Minutes tick by, but still, I don't dare move. Not even when something crawls over my bare foot or when my skin there begins to sting.

The lack of movement is rewarded when someone walks down the front porch stairs and stands on the last one. The shadow cast from the light behind them nearly touches me, and I wait with bated breath to see what they'll do.

Is it Titan? Does he suspect I've stayed behind, hiding? Or is it the man who gave me the chance to escape?

I don't know, and I refuse to move just to sate my curiosity.

Instead, the ground and the bug-infested bush become my haven for minute after minute until I can no longer track the time. People come and go, but nobody speaks, and I don't dare budge from my hiding spot.

At least, not until the door slams closed one last time and the light over the porch goes off. Another significant amount of time passes—what feels like hours to me—and there aren't any other sounds outside. It's still the middle of the night. Not even a hint of the morning sun is on the horizon. I don't know where I am or how I'm going to find help, but I know this is my chance.

I crawl out from under the bush and move my hands over my body, brushing away whatever unwanted friends have accumulated since my escape. I consider standing, but that seems like a bad idea when I'm still this close to the house. I continue to move on my hands and knees, making my way toward the neighbor's house.

Everything remains dark when I get to their fence, but still, I don't get back to my feet. I reach the next house over, this one without any kind of barrier around their yard. I check for movement around me before I fully rise from the ground, and once I feel as certain as I can, I start to limp through their backyard.

My entire body shakes with effort, and even though I'm ready to collapse into a bloody, soiled heap of nothingness, I focus on my steps. Left, right. Left, right. Left, right.

Each one takes me further away from Titan and closer to safety. I just need to find a phone and call...

Fuck me. The only person whose number I have memorized and might answer right now is Tori, and I can't call her like this. I can't allow her to be wrapped up in any of this, risking her life. Not when I know she'll want to take me right to the police, and something tells me that's not the right choice.

Even with my hope a little less buoyant, I manage to keep walking, and once I exit the backyard, I realize it leads right onto a golf course. The chance that I'm anywhere close enough to Luca's downtown compound lessens the moment I see the greens, but still, I don't give up.

I'm halfway across the eighth hole when my legs buckle. I can't hold myself up any longer. I can't take another step, not knowing what's coming next and if I'll make it to safety or if Titan still has men out looking for me and one of them could have eyes on me right now.

I just can't.

With my body spread over the grass, I close my eyes and just breathe. I've fought for so long already. I've given everything that I have to give. At least I'm not going to die in that basement. Out here, under the stars... It's not the worst way to go.

There's no doubt I have some sort of internal damage after the plethora of boots that found my body oh-so desirable, the hands that tossed me into walls, and the fists that marred my skin.

Maybe everything will just shut down and show me mercy.

As my breathing slows, there's a slice of regret that cuts through me. I promised to never give up, that I would fight for the happiness I deserve. Yet, here I lay. Unworthy of the life I've been given.

A whirring sound hums in the distance, and I lose my thoughts to the white noise until it turns into a horn. Two quick beeps that sound familiar...

My consciousness perks up. I'm still in Portland. I'm near a light rail station. That's the sound of a train I've taken dozens of times before. It has to be. That's what I need to believe right now. If I can make it to the stop, I can wait for the next train. Even if it doesn't come for several more hours, assuming that's a possibility since it's likely the middle of the night, I have no problems waiting.

The relief growing within me is a balm to my cracked spirit. I might be battered and bruised, but I'm not defeated.

I roll to my side and take a steadying breath as I stare down at the green grass beneath me. The dew covers my bloody palms, and I use the moisture in a pathetic attempt to clean myself up, but that only serves to smear things around.

Getting to my feet, I force myself to continue across the golf course. When I get to the edge, where I can see the train stop, I start to cry.

I'm going to make it. My father didn't break me.

6

OLIVIA

Relief surges through me as I near the hill that leads to my refuge, but it's as if the once-solid ground beneath me has transformed into treacherous quicksand. Every step forward feels like a battle, each inch gained an agonizing triumph. When the hill finally looms ahead, I don't hesitate to drop to all fours, a silent acknowledgment of my body's limit.

I plow my way through the dead, fallen leaves, a slow and laborious march. Broken branches claw at me, adding fresh scrapes to my battered skin. The tears on my cheeks aren't just a release of pain; they're born out of a fierce determination to conquer the odds.

What seems like an eternity later, I reach the summit, only to be confronted by an obstacle—a fence. My breath fogs the air in front of me as frustration boils over. "You've got to be fucking kidding me." My words hang in the cold night air, mingling with each puff of breath.

The prospect of climbing the chain-link barrier feels impossible, especially in my current state. Even standing upright seems like a monumental task as my limbs shake with the effort it takes to even breathe. Hell, maybe a broken rib has already punctured a lung. The thought makes the need to search for an alternative path seem beyond my depleted reserves.

I slump to the ground in a twisted kind of surrender. If I was tracking the rising and setting of the sun well enough between the moments I was passed out in that room, I've been gone three days and none of the sleep I had in that time was peaceful. Being here, under the starry night, laying on the cool ground that seems to help my achy body...I let my mind begin to drift off, surrendering to the torment I've endured and desperately need to heal from.

But then my imagination decides to tell me that the shadows moving around me could be one of Titan's men and I'm mere seconds from having my sorry ass dragged back to the basement and killed.

I jolt up from the ground with wide eyes and wince, hugging my ribs with both arms. "Damn it. This is such shit."

Forcing myself to keep going, I draw on the fleeting burst of adrenaline. Using a nearby tree as support, I gather my strength. Facing the fence, I stand on wobbly legs, surveying the obstacle before me. Climbing anything like this would be a feat for me even under normal circumstances; my current condition makes this an

Everest-level challenge. I fight through the haze clouding my vision, blinking furiously.

I know I can still do it with the right motivation, but getting started is proving harder than I like. My eyes cast up and down, then back before blinking several times. I can hardly see straight, but I'm pretty sure there's an opening in the chain link further down.

Hobbling toward it, my shoulders drop with relief as I grasp the cut fencing and glance around me. "Thanks to whatever asshole did this."

The homeless population is a bit out of control in Portland and not always a pleasant sight, but in this moment, their destruction is my saving grace, and I vow to try to be more helpful to their situation in the future.

I start to slip through, but with shitty eyesight, my depth perception is off, and I lean too close to one side. The torn metal grazes my side, ripping my shirt and gouging my skin. Blood mingles with dirt as I extract myself, my other hand joining the fray. "Just what I needed," I mutter, both exasperated and resolved.

The desire to throw a mini pity party for myself starts to surface until I see the light rail stop just a dozen yards from me. All woes are forgotten and, when I see a pay phone, I start to laugh at the absurdity of it. Something that I didn't even know still exists is going to help save my life.

I can call... Fuck. My earlier thoughts come rushing back to me. Tori's number is the only one I have memorized. Bringing her into this isn't an option. I'll just have to wait for the train as previously planned.

Painfully so, I make it to the stop and fall to my knees again before rolling over onto my side. Bloodied and bruised, smelling like literal shit with tattered clothes, I can't imagine I'm a pretty sight, but that's not something I can worry about now.

"Are you...okay?" a woman's concerned but also suspicious voice asks.

My eyes crack open, and the blurry vision of someone bundled up on a bench, clutching something to their chest is all I can see.

"I'm great," I drone. "Do you know when the next train is coming?"

She hesitates in answering. "About ten minutes."

"Where's it heading?" I force myself to sit up in an attempt to freak her out a little less. "Better yet, where are we?"

"Are you sure you're okay? Do you want me to call the police?" she asks, making my heart race for reasons unknown. "I'm a—"

"Please, don't," I implore, cutting her off. "It's just a rough night. If I can make it to the north side of town, I'll be able to get where I'll be safe."

"This is going south." I can hear the frown in her voice even if I can't see it clearly.

Fuck. I start to get up so that I can at least sit on the bench. I'll need to wait for another train, one coming from the opposite direction.

"Do you know the schedule? Like when one might be headed toward the north part of town?" I ask once I'm no longer afraid of falling over.

She moves closer, and I tense involuntarily. Short blonde hair, blue scrubs, and an oversized bag—her appearance finally registering before she bends down to pick something up from the ground. "I'm supposed to call the police. Ignoring your...situation could cost me my job." She hands me a piece of paper. "You dropped this."

I squint at the note, but my vision betrays me. "Could you read it for me?"

Her lips tighten in concern. "I hope I don't regret this." She recites a phone number, and something about it seems oddly familiar, like a memory just out of reach.

How did that get into my pocket?

"At least let me help you sit down and clean you up until my train gets here," she says, wrapping an arm gently around me.

I don't argue with her, mostly because my thoughts are still trying to piece together who the number could belong to.

"Do you want to call someone?" the kind woman asks as she opens her bag.

"I'd like to, but—"

Holy shit. Is that Luca's number? I remember my pants being tugged at as the stranger gave me instructions on how to get out of the house. Had he also given me a way to find help faster?

"Can you dial the number on this paper and put it on

speaker?" I ask with desperation in my voice. "I don't want to get it wrong or dirty your phone."

She's stayed close enough that I can see a soft smile rise on her oval face. "Sure."

I wait, my stomach churning with nerves. If this isn't Luca's number, if it's someone who wants to hurt me, I'm not sure what I'll do. Then, I wonder if I'm going to get this woman killed because I'm allowing her to help.

My hand smacks at hers before the phone starts to ring. "Block your number. I don't want anyone to be able to...call you back."

Or more accurately, try to track her down.

Her mouth forms into a hard line. "Listen, I know an officer. He'll protect you."

My head is already shaking. "No, please. Just use star-sixty-seven and call that number." At least I think that feature still works. If payphones still exist, I'm sure that does too. Then, I add, "If it's not who I hope it is, I promise to let you do more."

I'm lying through my teeth. I'll try to run if it's anyone other than Luca, Justine, or Jaxon that answers, but I'm not going to tell her that.

"My sister is a survivor of domestic abuse," she says compassionately. "You deserve better than this."

"I know. And I *have* better, I swear." Well, I sort of do. Luca would never lay a hand on me, but his world is still dangerous. Though, she doesn't need to know that.

When the phone starts to ring, I hold my breath,

waiting for the voice that I yearn to hear. When it's on the third ring, I start to lose hope.

My eyes close, and I lean my head back against the wall behind me. I'm nearly ready to cry when the voicemail starts.

"This is Luca Monroe. Leave a message."

It's short and clipped and very much Luca. I start to laugh and cry all at the same time as the woman next to me asks if I want her to hang up.

"Yes, but can you send that number a text?" I ask through my tears. "I promise it's safe now that I know who it is. Hell, you'll probably even be rewarded. Text him and say that I'm here with you and where we are. Please."

Luca might not answer a blocked number, but he should at least read a text from an unknown one. At least, I fucking hope so.

"And you would be?" she asks, voice lightly trailing off.

"Olivia. Tell him it's Olivia Raven."

7

LUCA

As we're headed home from the now-burning warehouse, I'm almost asleep thanks to the cocktail of adrenaline that's already wearing off. I'd prefer to keep searching for Olivia, but I'll be no good to her if we get a new address from the account information and I don't get some sleep.

My phone buzzes. I intend to answer it in case it's someone with information about Olivia, but I accidentally send them to voicemail after fumbling to get my phone out of my pocket.

I consider calling right back, but the number is showing up as blocked and I'm too worn out to care. If they have something important to say, I can listen to the voicemail.

I close my eyes again, and a minute later, my phone vibrates again. I assume it's from the call, and go to listen to the voicemail, but it's a text message that has my heart nearly pounding out of my chest.

Unknown: I'm with Olivia Raven at the light rail stop on Bybee Blvd. She's in bad shape and needs a hospital, but would only let me call you.

"Turn the fuck around," I boom through the SUV. "Get to Bybee Blvd right fucking now."

Damon doesn't ask why. Just spins us around in the middle of the road and hits the gas harder. "What part of Bybee?" he finally asks, making a sharp left turn.

Jaxon already has the map up on his phone, waiting for further instructions to assist Damon.

"It's the light rail stop there," I say as I call the number showing in the text back.

A woman's voice answers hesitantly. "Hello?"

"Give Olivia the phone," I demand, the urgency making my voice sharp, even if it's not aimed at her.

She doesn't reply to me, but I hear her softly speaking Olivia's name and some rustling, then the phone is picked back up. "She's not coherent. She really needs a hospital. I'm a CNA. I could—"

"You'll do nothing other than wait right where you are and make sure she's still breathing," I interrupt more harshly than I'm sure this woman deserves after calling me, but I can't control my emotions. Not when my mind is conjuring images of my beaten Raven.

"I will get her a doctor as soon as I have her," I say, only slightly calmer.

"Three minutes," Jaxon announces, then adds, "And I'm already texting Theo. I'll make sure he meets us at the house."

Theo is the doctor we call when we need things kept more private. He also stitched up my bullet wound. He better fucking be there.

I hear a groan through the phone and have to be careful with how tight I squeeze the device in my palm. "Is she okay?"

"Her vitals seem strong," the stranger says. "I think she's more exhausted than anything else."

I fucking hope so.

"Turning on Bybee," Damon says. I start to look out the window, but it isn't until we pass a golf course that I see the train stop.

Damon slams on the brakes, and I shove my phone into my pocket as I race out of the SUV. Every lengthened stride sends shooting pains through my body, but there isn't a damned thing in this entire world that could keep me from being the next person Olivia sees when she opens her eyes.

I see a woman on a bench beneath the awning where the train stops and start to panic when I don't immediately see Olivia, but she's on the other side of the stranger and I'm at her side in seconds.

My shaking hands, usually associated with control and destruction, cradle her battered face with the utmost gentleness. One of her eyes is practically swollen shut, deep bruising covers her previous perfect skin, and blood is crusted at her hairline.

Rage boils beneath my surface, but my touch remains delicate and careful. "Raven?"

The word leaves my lips with a heavy sigh behind it, as if I haven't been truly breathing since the moment I realized she was gone. I need to know who did this to her. I need to make them pay in the most gruesome way I can imagine, but more than that...

I need her.

Rage aside, the need for retribution will have to wait. My Raven needs me, and I'm going to be by her side until I know differently.

She groans, shifting slightly, and I suppress the urge to react to every nuance of her pain. The stranger speaks up, and for the first time, I acknowledge her presence. "She might not wake up without assistance."

My stare, hard and unyielding, meets hers. "I will take care of her."

She retreats only slightly, not as intimidated as I expect. "I'm just saying—"

"I know what you're saying," I cut her off, my focus solely on Olivia. "Thank you for helping her, but she is my responsibility now." I reach into my pocket, grabbing a roll of hundred-dollar bills and tossing it her way. "For calling me when she couldn't."

Without waiting for her response, I lean down to pick up Olivia, holding her reverently yet with urgency. Her body is lax, her injuries evident even beneath the layers of dirt and grime.

Jaxon is at the back of the SUV, holding the door open, his gaze riveted on Olivia's condition. The rage and concern in his eyes reflect only a portion of my own emotions.

None of us say anything as I get in, remaining extra careful with my movements so that Olivia isn't jarred more than necessary. Her vitals might have been fine when that woman checked them, but I've seen enough broken bodies in my lifetime to know that could change at a moment's notice.

The drive back to Roe compound is done calmly but with efficient speed. My eyes never leave Olivia's face as Damon and Jaxon discuss things I can't think about right now.

She's been beaten to hell. Her clothes are soiled, and I'm certain she's lost ten pounds in the time since I've seen her. My lips press to her bloodied forehead, and I close my eyes briefly, doing my best to remain thankful for having her in my arms.

As much as I want to continue the hunt for Titan— even more so after seeing what he's either done himself or had someone do to my Raven—I know she's going to need me more than my vengeance.

I abandoned her once before for that same reason, and I won't make that same choice again. At least not when the situation is as dire as it is now.

Damon pulls into the parking garage of the

compound, and I wait for the door to be opened for me again before I dare to move.

Jaxon is on the other side. "Theo is already upstairs, getting set up in your apartment. He's going to look at you, too."

As if I'm going to let the doc waste time on me when Olivia needs more help. I ignore Jax as I carefully exit the SUV, Olivia still in my arms.

My focus remains on her precious form, her bruised and battered face a stark testament to the horrors she endured. My lips brush against her forehead again, a gentle caress filled with a mixture of tenderness and fury.

Damon's voice reaches my ears, discussing something with Jaxon that I can't fully process right now. Olivia's presence consumes me, and I can't tear my eyes away from her for more than a fleeting moment.

I see only her, perfect and broken, her features marred by pain. Her weight seems to intensify, a consequence of my waning adrenaline no longer masking my exhaustion. But it's not just her physical weight; it's the weight of responsibility, the weight of love, and the weight of all that's at stake.

"You ripped open your stitches," Jaxon points out as we're walking toward the elevator. "You're letting Theo help you before you pass out from exhaustion and blood loss."

The fact that I know I have no other choice in the matter if I want to be there for Olivia when she awakens irritates the fuck out of me. Still, I don't say anything. I keep my focus on holding her in my arms and making sure I have enough strength to get her to the apartment.

No way in hell will I ask Jaxon or Damon to do so on my behalf.

Once we're in the elevator, I lean against the wall and adjust my hold. My skin is clammy, and I can feel the blood moving down the back of my leg, but I keep my focus as much as I can on Olivia's face. Seeing the dried crimson in her hair reignites my strength, reminding me that my job protecting her is far from over, even with her safe in my arms.

As soon as the doors open to the fourth floor, I make the final push to get into my apartment. The door is already ajar, and I turn sideways to get in with Olivia still in my arms.

There's a hospital bed already set up in front of the couch. On one side stands Markus, and the other is Dr. Theo Thomson, who moves to help me, but before I can think my actions through, I'm practically snarling at him not to touch her.

"I need to help her, Luca," he says gently, not moving his hands aways.

Since I'm well aware of this, I do my best to wipe the glare from my face as I settle her onto the bed. Once her head is on the small flat pillow and her body is stretched out, I know I should go sit down, but I can't stand the thought of leaving her side.

"Make sure she's in no immediate danger and then

stitch up Luc again," Damon says from behind me. "He ripped his stitches open and is bleeding all over his floor."

One quick glance at my feet proves his words accurate, but I don't give a fuck about the rug beneath me. I'll toss it out the damn window myself.

Theo doesn't look up from Olivia's body when he replies, "I'll take care of it." His fingers poke around her face, then around her neck before he forces her eyelids open and shines a light into her unresponsive eyes.

"She's breathing normally," he says, but frowns as he does so. "But I'm pretty sure she has at least one cracked rib, a severe concussion, and possibly a skull fracture. I'll need to take her to my office to get scanned to be sure."

"Bring your machines here," I reply swiftly. "She's not leaving this house anytime soon."

"Luca," he warns bravely, but I shake my head.

"I will buy you new machines if that's what it takes." I say, refusing to change my mind. "She isn't leaving this house, and if you suggest she do so again, you'll see what happens when I'm really fucking angry."

While I know it would be quicker, Titan is still out there and his job unfinished. Assuming Olivia escaped, she's safest remaining in this house and that's where she'll stay until I say otherwise.

My intense stare stays on Theo until I make sure my point has been made. Within the next minute, he's already on his phone, speaking urgently to someone about a delivery. When he's done, he looks back at me. "I'll be forced to close my office until I can get these machines back there. You'll owe me close to two-hundred grand in order to care for her here."

"Done. Just make it happen." I lightly squeeze her hand, wishing she'd open her eyes and tell me what the fuck happened and how she got to that train stop, but before I can say another word, my left leg buckles and I have to use the hospital bed to hold myself up.

Jaxon and Damon are right there to make sure I don't fall, each of them grabbing one of my arms. "Come on, Luc," Jaxon says. "Let him stitch you before you need a transfusion."

I don't fight them as they guide me toward the couch that's going to be ruined by the time we're done here tonight. Though, a mess in my apartment is the least of my worries at the moment.

Seeing Olivia's perfect blue eyes is the only thing I allow myself to care about, even when the doctor jams a needle into my leg harsher than necessary—retaliation for my earlier threat, I'm sure.

He'll fix me and Olivia, and then my hunt will resume. For every bruise Titan put on my Raven, I'll put three on his, and for the broken bones, he'll get bullets. Lots of fucking bullets.

8

OLIVIA

Waking up has never been so dreadful, as if I'm resurfacing from a dark abyss. It's not the pain that greets me first, but rather an unsettling numbness. My body is dead weight, and even though I'm trying to open my eyes, they're not listening to my command.

My mouth is dry, but my breathing is normal, which is the only positive thing I can find right now. I try to force my hand to move, but I'm pretty sure nothing happens.

Wherever I'm at, it's quiet and warm. The surface beneath me is soft, but not like a bed. It's more like a cushion, and I'm realizing now that I can't even tell if I have any clothes on. That's how numb I feel.

A darkness casts over the eyes that won't open, and I feel the pressure of someone...or something touching my hand. "Why hasn't she woken up again?"

It's Luca. His voice is scratchy, and he sounds furious,

which hurts my heart more than I expected. I want to tell him that I'm right here, that I can hear him, but the words remain trapped within my uncooperative body.

"I told you what would happen when I had to give her the sedative," an unfamiliar male voice says. "I can give her something to reverse the effects, but if she panics again, she could cause herself further injury."

Panics *again?* When the hell did I do so the first time, and why can't I remember that?

"Do it," Luca grumbles. "It's been two days. I can't wait any longer."

Two days since when? Damn it, I have so many questions.

"Put a hand over her chest in case she tries to sit up," the other voice says. "She needs to remain calm, or she could further injure her splintered rib."

Splintered rib... Oh, hell.

I'm probably in a hospital, and that's likely a doctor talking, but why? I try to remember what happened to me and why I could possibly have been unconscious for two days, but there's nothing there. At least not at first.

As my mind races, the flicker of a memory emerges, like a fragile ember threatening to fade away. It's painful. I'm crawling in grass, battered and bruised, and I'm terrified, but I don't know why. There's a woman, but she's kind. It's not her I'm afraid of. I need to think harder, further back to before I was hurt.

Sensations of frustration, almost rage, intensify within me, the inability to remember gnawing at my sanity. I want to scream, but my current state remains impervious to any command.

What the hell happened to me?

A glimmer of movement rouses my awareness, and I feel a twitch in my fingers. "Olivia?" Luca's voice, a blend of desperation and relief, reaches my ears. "Are you awake?"

"She might need a few minutes to get her bearings," the other voice says. "Don't push her."

I don't need to be able to see to know that Luca is glaring at whoever is with him, and the thought makes me grin. Oh, how I've missed that grumpy mafia king.

But why have I missed him? Where have I been?

I try to think of the last thing I remember. I was in the apartment. He was fighting intruders while I was locked safely away with a gun.

Wait... Someone showed up. He said he was going to take me to Justine.

Hands cup my cheeks, and I can finally open my eyes. Luca's face is right in front of mine, tension lines around his eyes and mouth. "Raven?"

"Luca," I say, but the single word burns through my throat and comes out rough.

Another man appears next to him, blond and wearing a charcoal-colored shirt. "Ms. Danes, how are you feeling?"

"Like I was hit by a train," I manage to rasp, my voice raw and foreign to my ears. "Why does it hurt to talk?"

"You just need some water," the stranger says, then adds, "Luca."

Luca's stare turns menacing. "I'm not leaving her."

The man I assume is a doctor sighs heavily, but steps away without argument.

"What happened?" I ask. "Vin took me, and I can't remember anything else."

Luca's expression turns grim. "Nothing else? Not where you were or who hurt you?"

Closing my eyes, I delve into the memories, grasping at fragments that threaten to slip through my fingers. Grass, pain, fear, a kind woman. I push harder, reaching further back, attempting to regain a sense of normalcy from before my world unraveled.

I shake my head as the other man returns, and he says, "Let's try to get you sitting up a little more so you can drink this." He moves behind my head, and I hear the whirring of a quiet motor as my head starts to rise. "I'm Doctor Thomson, and I've been taking care of you since Luca brought you back here."

When he moves to face me again, I offer a smile and the thanks he probably hasn't received yet, but likely deserves. I'm sure it's not an easy feat being the doctor to a mafia king.

"You suffered a pretty severe concussion," he says, "and your memory loss is likely your mind trying to protect you after your previous...panic."

I glance at Luca whose face is filled with more

tension than I can understand without knowing what happened. "What did I do?"

"Nothing that isn't expected after what that bastard put you through." His words are terse, but his touch on my arm is as gentle as ever.

"Who? Vin?" The more time that passes, the more annoyed I'm getting at not remembering.

Just as I think Luca is going to tell me, the doctor places a hand on his shoulder.

"She might need more time to heal before rehashing anything," he explains. "If she's not remembering, there's a reason."

Luca ignores him, though, and keeps his focus on me. "If you really want to know, I can fill in what I learned while you were gone, but only if you're sure."

The grim look on Dr. Thomson's face is the only reason I give any hesitation, but still, the unknown is going to drive me mad.

"Tell me."

As soon as the words leave my mouth, the doctor reaches for a syringe. "It won't be as strong as before because you've healed more, but if you lose control over your actions, I'll be forced to give you another sedative for your own protection."

I nod with understanding as Luca glares at the poor man who's only trying to do his job of keeping me safe.

When my gaze meets Luca's again, I take a steadying breath, eager to know what the hell has been going on.

"Titan Moretti had you for three days," he starts, but I don't hear anything else after that name.

The face of that monster inserts itself front and center in my mind. The way he stared down at me as he beat me, uncaring that he's actually...my father.

Oh, God.

"Did you know?" I ask Luca, interrupting whatever he was saying as the weight of the truth becomes too much to withstand.

"Know what?" His head cocks to the side, eyes pinched in the corners.

I glance at the doctor, unsure if I should reveal such a secret with an audience. Luca seems to catch on, though.

"Leave us alone," he says. "She's handling this better than before."

A little surprisingly, Dr. Thomson exits the room without another word.

When the door clicks closed, Luca cups my cheek. "Did I know what, Raven?"

"That Titan is my father?" I purposefully say it bluntly because I need to be certain of Luca's answer. I need to feel confident that he didn't know this whole time and hadn't been using me as Titan wanted me to believe.

His answer is immediate and almost disgusted. "No. How is that even possible?"

"Well, when two people have sex—"

He cuts me off, clearly not amused by my need for a little humor. "Not what I meant, Raven."

I try to shrug, but the action hurts too much to

complete. "I'm well aware, but I don't have an answer for you. He left me and Mom years ago without a word. My mother had her secrets, and she always held out hope that he'd return, but I never understood and can't exactly ask her now."

Luca's entire demeanor softens. "I know and I'm sorry for that, but I'm even more sorry that son of a bitch is your father."

"You and me both." I frown. "Am I terrible for wishing him dead?"

His eyes move over my body, and his chest practically rumbles. "After what he did to you, no. Which is good, because he's going to die, regardless of what you want. The moment he let someone put a hand on you, he signed his death sentence."

As heartbroken as I now remember being that my own father had not only allowed me to be physically harmed, but beat on me himself, no amount of wishing for different circumstances can change the reality.

My father needs to die. Not only for what he's done, but for what he may do in the future. I have no clue what kind of shady shit he's into, and I don't really care to know at this point, but I can't imagine it's any good.

Luca leans closer and presses his forehead to mine as he breathes me in. "I thought I was never going to see you again."

I tense for a moment, wondering how many people he killed in the process of trying to find me, then I realize that the number doesn't really matter to me. Not now.

Not when I've been attacked twice and know this world is more fucked up than most people can comprehend. If Luca wants to go around killing those who hurt other people, me included, then he has my blessing. Hell, I'm feeling a little murder-y myself.

Those thoughts are quickly dashed away as his lips brush against my cheek. "I thought I would never get to smell you again."

His voice is gravelly and intoxicating, and I suddenly can't move a single muscle for fear that any action on my part will break whatever magic is happening right now.

Luca's gaze meets mine, and it's as if his eyes can see straight into my soul right now. "I thought I would never get the chance to properly taste you." His nose brushes against mine as he briefly closes his eyes. "I lost control without *you*."

He'd told me before that he wouldn't kiss me because he didn't want to "lose control." Had I been disappointed to hear that? Absolutely. Had I realized his childhood was a lot more fucked up than mine and he could have his weird quirks without judgement from me? Also, yes.

Yet, his confession ignites a spark of courage within me. This man, who has fought against his own demons, deserves to be free from the constraints he's placed upon himself. With my heart racing, I offer a small smile, a silent invitation.

As if understanding my unspoken request, Luca's gaze darkens, his yearning laid bare. The weight of his emotions, the wildness within him, all converge as his lips draw nearer to mine. In this fragile moment, the way my heart feels as if it's about to beat right out of my chest, I'm certain that regardless of my broken state, everything is about to change for the better. I'm certain that barriers are breaking down, that Luca is so close to allowing himself to fully embrace this connection.

I surrender to my growing emotions, hoping that Luca can do the same, to know that granting himself this chance at happiness is not a betrayal of his prior convictions, but a triumph over them. As our breaths mingle, I wait for him to make the move, to accept that letting me in fully won't be the end of his world because he needs this more than me.

This is Luca's moment, and I'll wait right here as long as he needs me to.

9

LUCA

Seeing Olivia open her eyes and being able to hold her again was everything I'd been hoping for since I realized she was gone. But hearing her speak, watching the emotions cross over her face the moment she started to remember what happened to her, and then hearing that Titan is her father... It's all too much to contain. The tight grip I've clung to, concealing my emotions, shatters as if fragile glass.

In this moment, I want nothing more than to kiss her, to hold her close, and to vow to shield her from a world that's harmed her more than enough, especially by the man who's passed on being her parent. Pressing my forehead to hers, I acknowledge that I can't keep my emotions locked away any longer. I'm losing control over the tight hold I've kept on them. The chains I've secured around my heart over the years have slowly been loosening in Olivia's presence. Each millimeter of restraint gone is replaced with how deeply I've grown to care for this woman.

Not only does she deserve better, but I won't live the rest of my life keeping people at a distance just because of the world I have immersed myself in.

I have to claim this woman in a way I refused to allow myself to do before. I need her to know that I'm all in now. That I won't push her away again. That I won't keep her in the dark. That for as long as she wants to remain by my side, she will be cherished and cared for in every way that I know she deserves.

My lips move from her cheek to her mouth, hovering over hers with only a hairsbreadth of space between us. She stays completely still, not moving closer or further away from me, allowing me to make this choice as if she understands what it means to me. Even if I'm not entirely sure myself.

I've always been strong-minded and excelled at the tasks I chose to focus on. There was only once that I allowed myself to care for another enough that I became wild. A consequence that I suffered from when her father took her away from me once he learned who my family really was.

It had been teenage lust, but real emotions to me at the time. My father hadn't let it pass by without teaching me a lesson in life. It was beaten into me until he deemed me strong enough to withstand foolish emotions such as love.

I didn't know better at the time and accepted his

words, using them to become who I needed to be to make sure nobody had the power to hurt me again.

Yet, by denying myself the intimacy of kissing Olivia, by resisting her fully, I've only reaped regret, especially while she was gone. I can't afford any more regrets. I want her, and if she's willing to give herself to me, I'm done holding back.

My lips meet hers, gently at first, a cautious exploration that ignites a tremor down my spine. She responds, parting her lips in a breathless sigh, a soft gasp carrying the promise of desire.

Her fingers, delicate and seeking, find the fabric of my shirt, clutching the cotton as if anchoring herself in the whirlwind of emotions as our tongues tangle, tasting each other until I can't tell where her mouth begins and mine ends.

Moving in closer to her, my heartbeat echoes in the space between us, a rhythm matching the urgency of our kiss. I taste her, every essence and flavor of her that I've come to crave. The warmth of her breath mingles with mine, creating an intoxicating blend that encourages me to keep devouring her.

As the kiss deepens, a fierce longing takes over, a primal need to be closer, to claim not only everything that she is, but what she will be. My body leans over her, instinct tempting me to cover her completely, to shield her from the world's harshness. But the ache in my bones reminds me of her fragility that I'm determined to protect and heal.

With a gentle yet urgent motion, I continue to kiss her as if our lives depend on the single action, my hand sliding around the curve of her head until my fingers entwine with the silky strands of her hair, keeping her as close as I feel comfortable doing without hurting her.

I can feel her heartbeat against my chest, a frantic rhythm that mirrors my own. Every breath, every desperate touch fuels the fervor between us. Our connection, one I've tried to keep at arm's length until now, is an inferno of emotions that burns away the doubts and fears, leaving only the raw and unadulterated truth of what we share.

It's more potent than the thrill of the hunt, more promising than my empire's success, and more certain than the family I've been building with the people closest to me.

As I finally draw away, breathless and craving more, I meet her eyes, my gaze an unspoken promise. The intensity of the moment lingers in the air, a heady cocktail of longing and devotion that has reignited a spark between us, a spark that now blazes with the potential of something more profound than I previously thought I could allow myself.

Her smile nearly knocks me on my ass until she speaks. "That was unexpectedly...pleasant."

"Pleasant?" I repeat, gripping the back of her head tighter. "I'm *pleasant* to you?"

Her cheeks flush crimson, and she pulls her lower lip between her teeth. "Oh, you're much more than that and you know it."

I loosen my hold and kiss her forehead. "I do. Now, tell me how you're feeling, so I can decide if Theo needs to leave or not."

"Theo?" she questions.

"Dr. Thomson, as he introduced himself."

"Ah." Her eyes roam over her body, and her hands move lightly over the sheet covering her lower half. "Before we get to that, how am I clean if I've been unconscious?"

"Justine took care of you while I was being stitched up," I say, trying to keep the annoyance out of my tone that the redhead had taken that job from me, but I wasn't in any shape to do so myself.

A crease forms between Olivia's brows. "Stitched up? Why?"

"I was shot the day we were attacked," I answer, rubbing my thumb over the back of her hand. "While I was busting down doors to find you, I tore my stitches."

"Vin told me that when he took me," she admits. "I wasn't sure if it was true after the fact and hoped it wasn't. But you're okay now?"

I nod, briefly stroking her jawline with the back of my fingers. "Now that you're back."

She leans into the touch, then reaches for the water she hasn't finished. "I still feel swollen. I want to ask for a mirror, but I'm afraid to see what I look like."

"Titan will pay for every bruise he put on your precious body," I snarl, then ask what I've been dying to know. "How did you escape?"

Her eyes widen, and she nearly chokes on the drink she's in the middle of. "I can't believe I forgot about that."

"Forgot about what?" Tension knots in my shoulders, climbing up my neck.

"There was a man there," she says. "I never really got a good look at his face, and he had no problem beating on me, but I'm pretty sure he was never as harsh as the others. He came the night I left and told me Titan was going to kill me and that I needed to run. He slipped your number into my pocket and told me how to get out. Even let me stab him to do so."

My mind reels as she talks. Who the hell is this man, and why would he do anything to help me? I don't know, but I'm going to fucking find out. I don't know a single person on Titan's crew, and this makes me feel as if Olivia getting free is a trap we might not be prepared for.

I squeeze her hand tighter, doing my best not to show my darker thoughts when I should just be grateful that she's not dead. Not worried about further attacks. Not for today, at least.

"I'll kill them all, regardless," I say, then glance down at her ribs. "How is your breathing?"

"A bit of a struggle, but I don't feel like I'm dying." She laughs darkly. "At least, not anymore. I was pretty sure someone was going to find my corpse on that golf course for a minute there. And if that lady hadn't been at the train stop...I don't know that I would have found my way back to you."

"I never would have stopped looking for you," I say, my tone more aggressive than I intend, but the thought of never seeing her blue eyes again drives me to near madness.

Her face softens, and she reaches a hand up, cupping my cheek. "And that's one of the reasons I'm still here and not running away screaming. As insane as all this is, having hope that you were out there looking for me is what kept me from giving up some moments."

The need to wrap my arms around her and squeeze is strong, but I ignore the desire, knowing I'm more apt to hurt her than anything else.

She tries to sit up higher in the bed and winces. I stand to move behind her and help just as Theo walks back in without knocking. I'm tempted to fire him out of spite, but I don't know what I would have done without his help. He might not get the politeness he deserves from me, but he'll at least be paid handsomely.

He goes straight for Olivia, smiling as he seems to be inspecting her face. "Do you mind if I check your vitals, Olivia?"

She shakes her head. "Do whatever you need, and then maybe I can get out of this bed?"

"Sure," Theo replies as he grabs her wrist. "Walking in moderation will be essential to your recovery over the next few days, but nothing beyond this apartment until it doesn't take all of your energy to cross the room."

The doc finishes his examination, and I stay out of his way as much as I'm capable of given the situation. He doesn't say much as he listens to her heart and lungs, then pokes around the ribs, then, when he's done, he steps back and smiles.

"I think my job here is done," he announces. "As long as you promise to take it easy, I'll leave the two of you to take care of each other. Luca shouldn't be doing much of anything, either, until that bullet wound heals properly. Whatever you did to make it worse tripled your healing time."

The consequences of searching for Olivia mean nothing to me. I would do it all over again if I had to.

Theo shakes my hand and nods at the equipment scattered through my living room. "I'll have people here sometime this evening to pick everything up. If you feel like you need the hospital bed a while longer, then keep it. That's easier to replace than the rest of this stuff."

I glance at Olivia, but she's already shaking her head. "He can lift me in and out of the bed just fine. I need a real mattress after sleeping on the ground for however long I was gone."

My teeth grind together at the image of her on the floor, beaten and bloody. I might have locked her in a cage, but I at least gave her a mattress and never laid a finger on her. Well, mostly.

A few days locked away, healing with Olivia, and

then I'd be back on the streets, hunting my prey. Well, as long as Damon, Jaxon, and Markus don't find Titan first, based on what Olivia remembers.

Though, something tells me that fucker fled the moment he realized his leverage had slipped away.

10

OLIVIA

Once Theo leaves, I suggest to Luca that we move to the bedroom. The allure of a comfortable bed, surrounded by warm blankets, is irresistible. And, if I'm honest, the thought of resting in Luca's arms, cocooned in his protective embrace, seems pretty damn perfect.

Luca lifts me with the utmost care, his movements practiced and gentle, avoiding any jarring as he navigates the doorframe. As he places me on the bed, I grasp his shirt, tugging him closer until our gazes lock in a charged moment.

I won't soon forget that first kiss, and while I have no intention of pressuring him for more than he's willing to give, I won't pass up an opportunity for closeness if he's open to it.

"Raven," he growls, a note of warning that contrasts with the twitch at the corner of his mouth, revealing his softer side that he often hides.

"Yes?" I reply, fluttering my lashes with feigned innocence.

"You need to rest," he insists.

While his concern is valid, I counter with, "I need you. I need to know that I'm safe, and having you right here will do that."

He doesn't lean in for another kiss, disappointing me only slightly, but he doesn't pull away either. It's progress, and for now, that's enough.

"You are safe," he assures me, his voice like a warm blanket on a cold day. "There's a new security system in place around the compound, and if we're ever attacked again, I won't leave you alone. Nobody will take you from me again."

That last bit makes my heart race. He wants to keep me. He didn't know that my father is Titan. He hasn't been using me this whole time.

The relief that I get from knowing those things are true is exactly what I need after the torture I've endured.

"Lay with me," I say as I let go of his shirt.

He stands and glances toward the living room. "I need to get my phone. I'll be here with you as long as you need me, but I need to keep the others informed of what you know. Tracking Titan is second only to making sure that you're okay."

A grin tugs at my lips, a realization dawning on me — my fierce, enigmatic mafia king actually cares about me.

"Is there something amusing about what I said?" he questions with a raised brow.

My smile grows bigger. "You like me. Like *really* like me."

His gaze darkens as he looms over me. "And so what if I do?"

"You don't frighten me." I push feebly at his chest. "Just admit it and get your ass in this bed."

He doesn't retreat. If anything, he leans closer. "Do you believe that gives you power over me, Little Raven? Do you think that just because I care for you that you don't need to be afraid?"

Without backing down, I raise my chin and keep his heady stare. "I do. Very much so."

There's a stretch of silence between us. Neither of us gives an inch, and the longer our gazes stay connected, the more my heart races and skin tingles.

"Good," he finally murmurs in a low tone, his voice thick with an edge. "But you're not entirely correct. Yes, you have power over me, but it's a power that makes me more dangerous. Do you know how many lives I took searching for you? How many more would have been struck down if you hadn't managed to escape?" His eyes search my face as he speaks with such certainty. "I won't change who I am, and I won't apologize for what I'm willing to do to protect you now that I have you."

The admission resonates within me, his words igniting a fire in my chest. I'm both exhilarated and awed by the intensity of his emotions.

"And *that's* supposed to scare me?" I ask with genuine curiosity.

His forehead nearly touches mine as he replies, "It should, but maybe it wasn't just innocence that drew me to you all those weeks ago. Maybe there's just enough darkness in you for this to work."

"Maybe so, which is good, because I have no intention to expect you to change or ask you to apologize for who you are," I reply, since something tells me that's important for him to know. "Now, go get your phone and get back in here."

He shakes his head as he takes a step back, a hint of amusement dancing in his eyes. "I gave you an inch. That doesn't mean you need to take a mile."

I chuckle, feeling lighter than I have since that day in the garden. "Pretty sure you gave me much more than an inch and I took every thrust without complaint."

Luca's adorable groan follows him out of the bedroom, and I continue to grin. I was nearly dead last night...well, two or maybe three nights ago. I can't remember how long they said I was unconscious, but the life beating inside me now, pushing all the darkness I endured down, is what I need.

I can deal with the trauma later. Right now, I just need some fucking happiness in my life, and I'm going to seize every moment I can while it's right in front of me.

Fuck my father. Fuck the bruises that cover my body and the fractured rib. Fuck every ache that lingers.

The choice is mine to move forward, to tell Luca anything and everything I can remember, and hope like hell he finds Titan. Even more so, I hope he'll let me be there when it's time for the son of a bitch to die.

He was right before. I felt that thirst for blood when I saw the man who attacked me in the club tied to the chair in Luca's dungeon of death...or basement. And I feel it now. Seeing Titan pay for not only what he's done to me, but to my mother, would bring me insurmountable joy.

I only wish I could talk to her now and ask her if she knew who her husband really was. Had he been in touch over the years? Did he leave to keep us safe? That last one is a nice thought, and something tells me that's what he may have told my mother to pacify her, but I don't believe it. After what I've seen, he's nothing more than a selfish bastard.

Luca returns with his phone in hand and heads into the closet. When I can't see him any longer, I call out. "Whatcha doing?"

"Changing."

His tone is clipped, so I don't say anything else. Instead, I take a moment to appraise the damages to my body. I assume that when Justine cleaned me up, she also put the clothes on me. Though, the button-up, ultra-soft, green cotton shirt and matching shorts are nothing I previously owned.

Pushing back the covers, a constellation of aging bruises graces my thighs, and when I lift my shirt to see my stomach, there's more of the same, just bigger, thanks to Titan's swift right foot that seemed rather fond of my midsection. To be honest, I'm surprised I only have one broken rib. I expected much worse.

And the bandage on my left side, presumably from the gouge caused by the fence, I can only blame on myself.

I should probably ask for a mirror to see my face, but with how well I'm handling all of this, I decide it's best to wait. My jaw is sore, my eyes still burn—I assume from being swollen—and I can feel a scabbed-over cut at my hairline. Whatever is there, I'll let my imagination conjure an image, likely nowhere near as bad as reality.

Luca walks out of the closet dressed only in loose grey cotton pants and I can't take my eyes off him. The deep V at his waist has my eyes drawing further south and my tongue darting out. The desire to explore his body rips through me, causing an ache between my legs that I'm not sure there's anything I can do to sate. I'm under no assumptions that he's going to touch me however I might need until I no longer look like death.

Still, that doesn't mean my mind can't conjure images of our previous encounters, the way his tongue works its way down my body before lapping at my clit as if it was the last source of nourishment in existence.

Before I can work myself up too much, I squash my inner desire as best I can, then attempt to turn my body toward him, but even that small movement makes me wince.

Yeah, we're at least a couple days from sexy time.

His hard stare turns on me. "If you keep looking at

me like you were and you're not careful, I'll be sleeping on the couch."

That's a threat I'm going to heed.

"Then, come closer so I don't have to move," I say, hoping he's still in the mindset of not denying me. I intend to take full advantage of it while I can, to the point that doesn't have him sleeping anywhere besides next to me.

He slides into the bed, his lower half under the comforter, and moves until he can wrap his arm around me. My head leans against his side. "I hate to push you, but I need to ask about where you were. We thought we had a lead with a bank account number, but that turned out to be a dead end."

Ah, no wonder he was pissy when he walked back in.

I start to recount what I remember of the house and its surroundings, but I'm only able to utter a few words before a knock at the door interrupts us. Justine's voice filters through the room.

"Well, if you would have told me the moment she woke up, I wouldn't have to barge in."

Even though I can't see them from the bedroom, I picture Jaxon's annoyed expression and Justine's determined stride, which makes me smile again.

I reach for Luca's hand and squeeze. "Don't tell her to go away, please."

"She's lucky you like her," he grumbles in reply and surprises me when he stays in bed.

Justine knocks on the door frame. "Everyone decent?"

"No," Luca replies curtly. When I give him a glare, he adds, "You said not to tell her to go away. Not that I had to be nice."

He makes a point. Before I can amend, Justine and Jaxon walk in, the latter with an apologetic look on his face. "I tried to stop her."

"Clearly, not very hard," Luca says, then moves his hard stare to Justine. "Today is the exception. Don't ever come into my room again without permission. Do you understand?"

Justine is at least smart enough to nod without the cocky grin I'm sure she's holding back. "Understood."

Jaxon glances between Luca and me. "Did you get the location?"

"She was just telling me when we were rudely interrupted." Luca looks down at me. "What do you remember, Raven?"

"There's a residential area beyond the golf course behind the light rail stop," I say, then frown. "I didn't see any street names, but if I have a map, I might be able to get close. I do know that the house was at the end of a cul-de-sac with a white porch and a massive hydrangea bush on the left that I hid under."

Jaxon is handing me his phone before I'm even finished speaking, and the golf course is in view. Using two fingers, I zoom in and out while moving the map around. Damn it. With how dark it was when I left and how freaked the fuck out I was...none of this looks familiar, but still, I keep trying.

Then, I remember the yard I escaped through. They didn't have a fence at that house, but most of the others did. Except the harder I concentrate on the screen, the more my head pounds. I hand the phone to Luca. "Find a house without a fence in a cul-de-sac that backs against the golf course," I tell him, closing my eyes and leaning back against the pillow.

"Are you okay?" he asks with an edge to his voice.

"It's just the screen. I'll be fine."

I feel the bed dip next to me. "I read up about concussions. You're not supposed to watch TV or be on the phone much for a while," Justine says, then grabs my hand. "You're really okay, though?"

My eyes open to peek at her, and I offer a smile. "As good as I can be. I'll be back to my old self in no time."

She reaches into the purse at her side, then holds up a small white jar with writing on it that I can't read. "I got this for you. It's supposed to help make the bruises fade faster and give you some relief from the pain."

"Thank you," I say sincerely as she sets it on the nightstand next to me.

Luca mutters a curse under his breath and is out of bed in the next second, handing Jaxon's phone back to him as he storms off. "Find that house, right fucking now."

I glance between Jaxon and Justine, confusion filling me. "What the hell just happened?"

Jaxon is already passing off the task of finding the house to Justine. "I don't know, but I'm going to find out."

The tightness in my chest makes my lungs burn, and my emotions threaten to get the best of me. Titan must have done something. Something bad enough that Luca doesn't want to tell me yet.

Justine lightly squeezes my thigh. "Everything's going to be okay. Let's just find this house, okay?"

I nod, trying to believe her, but not succeeding in the slightest as the echo of the slamming door vibrates through the apartment.

11

LUCA

As if safeguarding Olivia hasn't been stressful enough, now I'm faced with the added concern of those closely tied to her. This is the last damn thing we need. I slam the apartment door shut with unnecessary force, rereading the text message that has just arrived.

Damon: Tori called the police to report Olivia missing. Titan apparently has contacts there as well and he got her.

Olivia is going to lose her mind when I tell her, something I don't want to do. Especially when it seemed as if she was content to keep her friend at arm's length when it came to what happens in this house.

"Fuck!" My voice reverberates in the empty landing as I clench my phone, dialing Damon's number instead of bothering with a text.

Jaxon joins me, his posture reflecting the tension in the air. "What happened?"

I raise a finger, silencing him as Damon answers the phone. "This is not good."

"No fucking shit," I snap. "Someone had to see who took her, what they were driving, and what direction they went. Give me something, Damon. I can't just tell Olivia that her friend is missing without a single fucking lead."

Jaxon lets out a low whistle as I wait for Damon to reply.

"A guy that's not popping up on facial recognition put her in the back of a black BMW," he says. "They turned onto Madison, heading toward Hawthorne Bridge, and we lost them from cameras after that."

My fist slams into the wall next to me, leaving an imprint of my knuckles. "Find her. Search for her like we're looking for Olivia."

This woman means nothing to me, but I know she's everything to Olivia, which makes her something. I might not go on a murder spree to find Tori, but I'll give her all my resources and then some.

Damon confirms he and Markus are on it, then hangs up. Jaxon is still waiting there with me but doesn't say a word until I turn to face him.

"I didn't see this coming."

"Neither did I." My lips flatten. "Since Olivia woke up this last time, she's been calm and even playful. Nothing like the frightened woman she was when she first woke up, screaming about Titan and thinking we were trying to hurt her. But this? Her best friend being taken? It's going to break her."

Jaxon reaches for my shoulder and levels his stare on me. "Give her the benefit of the doubt, Luc. Maybe she'll surprise you."

"Yeah. Maybe, but I need to prepare for mayhem." It's one thing for me to rage, but I'm not sure what I will do with Olivia if she falls apart.

Even when I basically kidnapped her, she remained strong. It was just another thing that drew me to her, her unwillingness to give in to the fear whenever I loomed over her, slowly burrowing under my skin. Seeing her as anything else...

I know nothing about handling a frantic woman, and this seems like a situation that she's apt to lose her shit over. Worse, Olivia is going to blame herself and I can't fix that.

"You can't control every little thing," Jaxon says, and not for the first time throughout our friendship.

"But I can certainly fucking try." I turn to head back into the apartment, but I still don't know what I'm going to tell Olivia.

The thought of keeping this from her until I know more is preferable, but from what I already know of Olivia...she'd have my balls once she found out.

Though, her being angry with me is better than her falling apart. Maybe that's the right call.

"Go tell her," Jaxon says. "The sooner, the better. Then, we can get back out there and find her friend."

My chest rumbles with tension. He's right, even though I'm not ready to admit it.

I lead the way inside and head back toward the bedroom. I'm halfway across the living room when my phone starts buzzing. Damon's calling back already.

"News already?" I answer.

"Sort of," he replies cautiously. "I was leaving the garage and saw an envelope taped to the gate."

Motherfucker.

He continues. "It's a demand. Olivia for Tori."

I should have seen that coming. My grip tightens around the phone, threatening to crack the thin device. "Use the security footage. Find out who left the note and use whatever means necessary to track where they went when they left here. Bribe, threaten, hack. I don't give a shit what you have to do. Just fucking find where they have her."

We had to soon, because Olivia would absolutely trade herself to save her friend. I know that without a doubt in my mind.

"You still have to tell her," Jaxon says, standing close enough that I know he heard the entire conversation.

"I know." I take a deep inhale, then slowly exhale before proceeding to the bedroom.

The fucking bruises haven't even healed on her face, and from the sounds of it, Titan had intended to kill her before she escaped. Why does he...

I turn to Jaxon as another thought occurs to me. "I need to know who the inside man is that let Olivia escape. She stabbed him. If Titan doesn't have his own doctor on call and didn't want his guy to bleed out, he would have gone to the ER. Call around about stab victims, figure out his name. Now."

Why the thought hadn't occurred to me before is beyond me, but if this elusive man helped us once, maybe he'll help us again. Whoever he is, he just might be our ticket to getting Tori back. That's the idea I needed to feel not so uneasy about telling Olivia.

When I walk into the bedroom, Justine has taken my spot on the bed, but instead of demanding for her to get out and further upsetting Olivia, I ignore her and move to the other side of the bed to sit next to my Raven.

She licks her lips and looks up at me with trepidation. "What happened? What did Titan do now?"

"He took Tori," I say bluntly.

Olivia sucks in a breath, and her eyes gloss over as if she's about to burst into tears, but within seconds, she reins it all in and her mouth twists in a snarl. "I'll fucking kill him myself if he hurts her."

Jaxon's suppressed chuckle drifts in from behind me. "Told you."

Without acknowledging his needless comment, I ask Olivia about the stranger. "Are you sure there's nothing you can remember about the man who helped you escape?"

The crease between her brow deepens. "What does that matter?"

"If we can figure out who he is, then he might be

willing to help Tori do the same." And if he doesn't, I'll kill him right alongside Titan regardless of his good deed in letting Olivia go.

I watch her face as she processes the idea and, even though her eyes soften, there's still a murderous lilt to her tone. "He better fucking help her." She closes her eyes for a moment as I assume she's attempting to remember anything helpful. When she huffs a few seconds later, I already know what her next words will be.

"I have nothing, but we did find the house," she says, and the latter takes me by surprise. "I'm sure of it."

Justine hands me the phone and points at a grey house with white trim, shown from a street map view. "That's it right there."

Jaxon takes his phone and is already walking toward the door. "I'll call the hospitals on my way to check it out."

As much as I didn't want to leave Olivia so soon, I can't let Jaxon walk into an ambush. Titan would know that we'd want to check out the place where she was being held first.

"Wait," I demand, then grab Olivia's hand. "I'm going to lock you and Justine in this room. Do not open that door for anyone other than myself, Jaxon, Damon, or Markus. They're the only people you can trust."

She nods and squeezes my fingers tightly between her own. "Call me the second you can after you get to that house."

"I will." I lean forward and kiss her forehead, then

move to get dressed again, opting for my last clean pair of black jeans and a black shirt. My preferred color to hide my favorite one: crimson.

Once I'm finished and armed, I give Olivia one last look. She's holding herself together better than I predicted, but I suspect there will still be a point in which she falls apart. A person can only be so strong, and she's been through hell since the moment her mother died only a month or so ago.

Her eyes follow me across the room, and she nods as if giving me permission to do whatever it takes to get her friend back. Not that I wouldn't have anyway, but at least I know she's not disgusted by what I do when necessary.

Jaxon is waiting at the door, and when I close it behind me, I activate not only the alarm that will screech through the house if the lock is tampered with, but also the electricity that will shock whoever tries to touch the door to their near death.

Worth every bit of the hundred grand I paid for it.

"The house is about fifteen minutes from us, and I already called the first hospital, using the fake badge number they never bother to check," Jaxon says with a bit of pride. "Only one stab victim in the last seventy hours and it was a woman."

"I'll drive while you keep calling," I reply, entering the elevator and pressing the button for the garage. "We need to get Tori back."

"Or your girl is going to go on a killing spree just like

you," he jokes, but I have a feeling he's not far from the truth.

My Raven may not have taken a life before, but something tells me the glimpses she's already had of my world have shown her that she's not as opposed to murder as she may have previously thought.

12

OLIVIA

There's a small part of me that is terrified for Tori, but my inner fury is like an inferno, growing inside me and taking out everything else in its path. The fact that I'm bound to this bed only adds gas to the flames.

Never in my life have I wished someone dead like I do Titan right now. Even more so, my fingers itch to be the one to take the life from his eyes. It's one thing for him to go after me because I refused to be the daughter he wanted or give him info on Luca. It's an entirely different thing for him to take Tori.

She's been in my life since before he left, so she knows him. She may even trust him at first. Not knowing what he's doing to her makes me crazier by the second.

Justine reaches for my hand, forcing my fingers to unclench. "Easy there. You're going to hurt yourself."

"I'm already fucking hurt," I retort darkly.

"Luca will find her," she assures me, attempting to pacify my escalating anger.

I shake my head, my doubt refusing to be subdued. "He couldn't find *me*."

The words escape before I can rein them in, regret instantly filling the space they left behind. It's not that Luca didn't try, not that he didn't exhaust every resource to bring me back. But the reality is that he *hadn't* found me. Titan stayed at least a step ahead of him the entire time.

I don't blame Luca for it. I'm well aware of how relentless he was in his search. But the bitter truth is, there's a possibility this could all go downhill again, ending in heartbreak. If I lose Tori...

It doesn't matter that I've found a family within this compound over the last month, that I trust and love Justine and that I know Luca would protect me with his own life.

Tori has been in my life for decades, and I've put her in danger by not only choosing to be here, but by keeping the truth from her. I should have trusted her with what I'd gotten myself into. If I had, then she wouldn't have been in a position to be taken. She could have...

I don't fucking know, but something. Hell, she could have been here. With me.

Probably not, but I can't help blaming myself, imagining all the possibilities that could have prevented our current situation.

Justine reaches for the cream she brought. "Let's

focus on the things we can do. Like getting you better, yeah?"

Begrudgingly, I agree. The only way I'll be able to help Tori myself is if I can get the hell out of this bed. So, with that in mind, I let Justine cover my face and ribs in the lotion without further complaint.

When she's done, I actually do feel better. The soreness isn't as severe as it was only minutes ago, and I say as much.

"There's a bit of lidocaine in this stuff," she replies. "It helps numb the skin, but it doesn't mean you're healed."

Her last words are said sternly, but she doesn't intimidate me. At least, not today.

"Dr. Thomson said I could walk short distances," I tell her. "While I'm not feeling so sore, help me get out of bed."

Her eyes narrow at me. "Are you lying?"

"Call him yourself and check." I'm already trying to move my legs on my own. Damn it. Why does everything hurt so bad, and how the hell did I even make it to that train stop?

She huffs. "I believe you. Mostly."

Her hands wrap gently around my thighs, helping to get my feet off the side of the bed before she reaches for my shoulders to help me sit up.

As I'm lifted, my head starts to pound and my stomach churns, but I push down the nausea. I can't get sick, or Justine won't ever help me out of the bed. I need to be strong for Tori, just as I assume she's attempting to be for me right now.

"How are we doing?" Justine asks, still keeping a hold on my shoulders that I silently appreciate.

"Okay," I say. "I just need a minute here before we walk."

A smirk curls on her lips. "If you'd said anything else, I'd have known you were lying, so good choice."

"How?" I glance up, trying to act stronger than I feel.

Her finger pokes lightly at my forehead. "You're all sweaty and pale. Probably seconds from passing out if you do anything else. I'm going to help you, but not at the expense of your recovery."

Once again, I know she's right, but that doesn't mean I want to agree with her. I need to move. I need to...do something. Anything that will help get Tori back.

Being helpless is really fucking shitty.

"Can you sit up on your own?" Justine asks, staring hard at my face. "I think you need some water before we continue."

My palms press flat on the bed, and I nod. "I can sit here."

"And stay," she adds with a snicker as she heads out of the bedroom.

I'm tempted to get up out of spite, but I decide better of it. One thing worse than my friend jokingly treating me like a dog is falling on my face and having her find me ass-up on the floor. Though, it wouldn't be the first time...

She comes back with two bottles and some crackers.

"Take a few sips and try to eat something first. Theo gave you liquid sustenance while you were unconscious with an IV, but you haven't had real food since Luca brought you home."

Hell, I haven't had real food in a week. Titan only gave me water and a slice of stale bread a few times while he had me.

Now that I'm thinking about it, my stomach growls loudly and the crackers suddenly make me ravenous.

Justine laughs as I take them from her. "We'll get you real food as soon as we're done walking. You don't want to eat too much, only to throw it up."

Shit. I hope I don't vomit just from walking. That would mean I'm worse off than I feel. For now, I'm going to hope that little strolls and a lot of rest over the next day or two will have me moving normally enough that I can leave this apartment.

I'm what Titan wants, even if Luca hasn't said it. At least, that's what I assume since he took my best friend. If they can't find her, then I'll gladly be the bait to do so. Hell, I'd trade my life for hers. None of this has anything to do with her, and if I can save her life, then I'll do whatever it takes to do so. Consequences be damned.

After I've eaten and drank, Justine finally helps me to the ground. The numbing from the cream has increased, but not to the point that I can't feel my movements. Just enough that there's a chance I might overdo it without realizing, which I intend to be mindful of.

"Ready?" Justine asks as she keeps an arm wrapped around my waist and a hold on my hand.

I lift my foot and take the first step. "As I'll ever be."

"Girl, your strength baffles me. On top of the love I have for you, there's a healthy dose of respect," she confesses, surprising me with her compliment.

Another step. "Why would you say that?"

"I would be in a ball in the corner if I were you," she answers with a grimace. "I thought having a stalker take away my sense of security was bad, but that lasted for just a few days. What you've endured over the last month... it's more than most anyone could handle. So, no matter what happens next, just know that you're strong enough to withstand it."

It's almost like she's preparing me in case we don't find Tori, but I refuse to let that thought take root in my mind. We will find her, she's going to be okay, and Titan will die. Anything short of that is not an option I'm willing to entertain.

We make it across the bedroom and to the bathroom. I don't know if that was an intentional direction, but now that I can see the toilet, I'm thankful we're close.

"I need to pee," I announce with a chuckle. "And you're going to have to help me sit on the toilet."

She laughs alongside me. "As long as you don't ask me to wipe your ass, then we're good."

Even as my legs shake and my head sweats, I can't help feeling thankful for her friendship, especially in this moment. "You know you would if I really needed it."

She sighs but can't hide her smirk from me as she says, "Let's not find out, okay?"

"Deal."

As soon as I'm seated on the toilet, my phone starts to ring, and I swear my heart is seconds from breaking out of my chest because of it.

Justine leaves my side and rushes to answer. I can't hear what's being said as I move quickly to finish my business and flush, but when she re-enters the bathroom, she's holding the phone out. "It's Luca. He has some questions."

Fuck. I hoped he'd have good news, not more questions.

I take the phone and place it on speaker, so Justine can listen and I won't have to repeat the conversation later.

"Luca?"

"We found the house you were kept at," he says, voice neutral. "I went to the basement and the place has been scrubbed clean. I can smell the bleach."

Damn it. Why couldn't Titan be a cocky piece of shit who just stayed in one place?

"What can I do to help?" I ask, my desperation surfacing.

"Tell me more about your time here," he says. "Were the lights on? Did they bring you food at the same time each day? Did you see anything when they took you to the bathroom?"

Telling Luca that I pissed and shit near the door just

to annoy them isn't something I feel particularly comfortable with, so I avoid that question.

"The lights were on when I was alone and when Titan came in," I say, "but when anyone else would enter, they turned off. I think there were only two, maybe three others that came to...visit me. I never really saw their faces, though."

"How did you know they were different?" I hear Jaxon's voice ask.

"Because their beatings varied. One not as harsh as the others. I assume the stranger who helped me," I answer and can clearly picture the fury on Luca's face as a rumble echoes through the phone.

"Did Titan tell you anything to try and sway you?" Luca asks after a few seconds of silence. "Anything that would tell you what his plans were?"

I frown, hating that I can't be more helpful. "He only talked about what a terrible person you were and told me that you knew I was his daughter. That you've been using me this whole time to get to him. When I didn't believe him, he called me a whore and the beatings began. Anytime I saw him after that, he only asked one question: 'Have you changed your mind?' When I refused to answer, he retaliated."

"I can't wait to fucking kill him once and for all. I'm going to—" Luca cuts himself off as if attempting to hide his rage from me. It's not necessary and I start to tell him that, but he talks over me. "Thanks, Raven. We'll call back after we go to a couple hospitals."

"Do you think you found the guy I stabbed?" I ask, trying not to get too hopeful.

"A few potentials," he says, and I can't tell if he's optimistic about the leads or not. "I need to go. I'll call soon."

The call ends, and I look up at Justine from my spot still on the toilet. "This fucking sucks."

"It does, but we're doing everything we can, and if Tori is anything like you, then she's going to be just fine," Justine promises, but what she doesn't know is that my best friend is my complete opposite.

She's kind and soft and compassionate. Most of all, she's been thrown into this situation blind, giving Titan the perfect opportunity to manipulate her and use her against me.

I've never despised anyone more than I do him, but that rage is the strength I need to keep going. I didn't give up on myself, and I sure as hell won't give up on Tori.

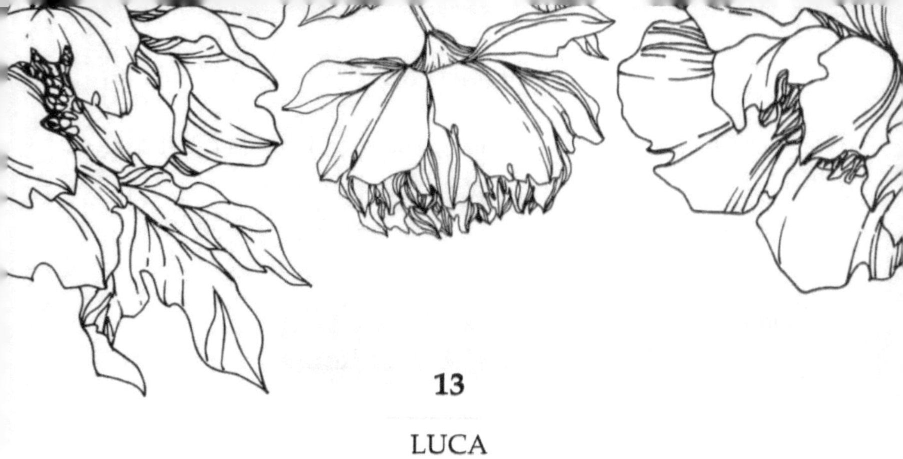

13

LUCA

The entire house has been scrubbed. There's nothing here other than furniture and decorations that were likely staged for whatever twisted reason Titan had.

Our next stop is the second biggest hospital in Portland and the closest one to where they'd been holding Olivia. If I had to go somewhere that I wanted to be busy enough not to ask too many questions and would also be convenient, that's where I would go. Considering this stranger who helped Olivia knows me, I'm hoping he also thinks like me.

Jaxon accompanies me inside the hospital, and together we approach the front desk of the ER center. A petite blonde staffs the desk, and Jaxon immediately turns on his charm.

"Well, hello there, beautiful," he purrs. "How's your day treating you?"

She blushes, and I fight the urge to roll my eyes. I'll let him enjoy his moment as long as it helps us gather the information we need.

"It's been busier than usual, but I'm hanging in there." Her smile is wide, and she leans slightly over the counter, resting her chin in her hand. Her gaze travels appreciatively over Jaxon. "I hope you're not here because you're hurt."

He moves closer to her and winks. "I'm made of steel. Nobody can hurt me."

I kick his leg, needing him to get to the fucking point already.

"But our friend," he says with a frown. "He isn't as blessed as I am. In both looks and strength."

Her brow raises as she continues to grin. "Well, isn't that too bad for him."

"It is because he ended up here a few nights ago and lost his lucky rabbit's foot."

Mother fucking hell.

Rabbit's foot? This is the last time I let him take the lead on anything.

"Hmm, I haven't seen anything like that laying around on my shifts, but I can go check the lost and found for you to see if someone turned it in," she says with a purr, then licks her lips. "You can join me to help identify it. You know, in case there are multiple to choose from."

"How about you just bring them all?" I say with a snarl that has her rearing back.

Jaxon shoves me out of the way, blocking me from view. "While I would love to, I should stay here and make sure this one stays out of trouble."

Her tone loses its sauciness. "Probably a good idea."

She gets up and goes through the door behind her. Before it's even closed, Jaxon is running around the counter and sitting in her chair.

"What the fuck are you doing?" I ask, voice laced with irritation that I'm certain he can't miss.

"Finding the name and address of the stab victims from the night Olivia escaped," he answers without looking up at me. "Unless I fuck that receptionist in the back room, she isn't going to break HIPAA laws. Not even for this handsome face."

Jesus Christ. He astonishes me sometimes.

"And clearly, I can't fuck her," he adds, droning on about shit I don't care about while he types. "Justine would have my balls cut off and bronzed. Shit, she might just for flirting with the woman. Those redheads, if you know what I mean."

"No, I don't," I mutter. "Now, how the hell do you know what you're doing?"

"The internet, Luc." He rolls his eyes at me like he's disappointed. "What did you think I was doing on my phone during our drive over here? I knew I needed to figure out the basics of the computer system they have here."

Well, now I'm a little impressed, but there's no time to tell him so, because another woman in scrubs walks through double doors on our left, and her narrowed eyes immediately land on us with suspicion. "Where's Miranda?"

Jaxon winks as if he truly believes he can flirt himself out of this situation that's bound to get the cops called on us. "She's in the back looking for my friend's rabbit's foot. Sweet girl, that Miranda. I bet you're a lot like her."

She reaches into her pocket and pulls out a phone. "Not even close. Don't move."

Before she can press more than a few buttons on her phone, I'm in her face, holding both of her arms firmly. "Listen to me carefully," I glance at her name badge, "Carrie. I need to know who the stab victims were three nights ago, and I'm going to find out one way or another. No matter what measures I need to resort to. So, be a good nurse and move on to your next patient instead of making that phone call."

Her chocolate eyes squint even further, and she lifts her chin. Though, I don't miss the trembling in her body. "Do you have any idea the amount of threats I get on a nightly basis? You don't scare me. Now, take your hands off me before I make you."

She's full of shit. Her bravado is all show, but still... Hurting women isn't something I do. Threatening them into submission, sure, but knocking this one unconscious so that Jaxon can finish his job and we can make a clean escape? I'm not thrilled about the idea. But this is for Olivia. I don't really have a choice.

As I raise my arm to knock her unconscious, another

nurse comes in, but this one isn't a complete stranger. "Luca?"

I swear the universe is trying to ruin my life. I don't know what I did to piss her off, but I need to fucking fix things before shit gets worse.

It's the woman who called me for Olivia from the train stop. Her surprised gaze shifts between me and her co-worker, then to Jaxon. "What's going on here?"

"I'm trying to find who hurt Olivia," I say, hoping she'll be sympathetic to the situation.

Her face doesn't soften like I hope. "Did you take her to a hospital like I suggested?"

"I had a private doctor attend to her," I say, not letting go of the woman in front of me in case the situation continues to get worse. "She's resting at home as we speak."

"Uh huh," she replies. "I did a little research on you, *Luca Monroe*. Something tells me that the media finding out you're assaulting nurses wouldn't be good for business."

I should have fucking killed her when I had the chance. I don't take being threatened lightly. It's the one thing I hate more than hurting a woman who doesn't necessarily deserve my wrath just because she's doing her job.

My hold remains on the quiet nurse as I stare down the other. "You work in the ER. You see plenty of people with ill intentions in here who don't deserve to be helped, but still, you save their lives. Just look the other way and let me do my job to save someone else's life. Olivia isn't the only one this person intends to hurt."

The woman in front of me tilts her head. "Are you talking about Olivia Danes?"

"How the fuck do you know who she is?" I sneer.

She swallows thickly, finally finding the proper amount of fear for the situation. "I don't know her, but I helped someone who does. He said if anyone came in looking for her that I was to give them a note."

"Who?" I demand.

But it's not the nurse that answers. It's Jaxon. "Bryson Holmes."

He has to be fucking shitting me. This situation just went from fucked to twisted with those two words.

Jaxon comes out from behind the desk and shows me a piece of paper with Bryson's name, address, and a list of the injuries from when he came in just a few nights ago, but I don't pay attention to that for long. My attention goes back to the nurse. "Where is the note?"

"In my pocket," she says. "He told me to keep it with me every day until someone came. He seemed rather certain they would."

Of course, he would be certain. That man was like an uncle to me until he disappeared after my father's death. I always assumed he had something to do with it, but never could find him. Not that I looked for long. A part of me didn't want to find and kill him.

I release her so she can grab the note herself. When she hands it to me, the paper shakes and she backs up to the nurse that saved Olivia, whose name I can now see is Sarah. Though, I've already forgotten the other.

Before reading whatever message was left, I know we need to get the hell out of there. I look at both women and nod. "I'm sorry for scaring you, but I didn't have another choice."

"And neither will we if we see you in here again," replies Sarah. "If you threaten anyone here a second time, the world will know about it. Please give Olivia my best."

Just as we get to the exit, the pitiful receptionist calls out, "Jaxon!"

"If you so much as turn around, I will put a bullet through your foot," I mutter as we walk through the automatic doors.

His hand clasps my shoulder, and he grins. "I take that as progress. You didn't actually threaten my life. Just a bit of blood."

"Don't start with me," I say as we get in the car. Only when he's driving away from the hospital do I open the single piece of paper.

It has the hospital's logo on the top, and there are a few drops of dried blood around the edge, but the words are legible, which is all I care about.

Luca,

I have no other way to reach you without compromising my position. I've spent years with Titan, trying to fix a mess that started with your father. I had no idea who

Olivia was until it was too late. I hope she survived.
Though, I'm sure I'll know if she didn't.
There's someone I still need to help, but if you want Titan
dead sooner rather than later, you're going to have to do so
yourself. We're headed to his last safe house tonight.
You've found all the others. I'll leave the address below.
Make your move soon. You have him scared. Even still, he
won't stop until he sees you bow to him with nothing to
your name.
Don't underestimate him, Little One.
Uncle B

I don't know how the fuck this is possible, and as much as I want to believe this is good news, there's something I don't like about this situation. If I'm to believe this note, Bryson has been working for Titan since my father died.

In all those years, he would have had more than enough opportunities to kill the son of a bitch. Plus, who could be more important to save over his own family? And what mess could he still possibly have to fix after all these years? I don't know the answers to any of my questions, but I'm damn well going to find out.

OLIVIA

I don't manage to stay awake long enough to witness Luca's return home. Despite my best efforts, the combination of walking, heating pads, and pain meds lulled me into sleep. Now, I'm awake, and the empty space beside me triggers more panic than I care to admit.

Without thinking, I sit up in bed, searching the room for any sign that Luca even came back. My head doesn't swim like it did yesterday, but there are still spots in my vision from the quick movement, so I pause and briefly close my eyes.

Once I feel more stable, I scan the room and notice his pants from the day before hanging out of the laundry chute in the bathroom. Well, at least he came home.

I slide slowly off the bed, careful to keep a hold on the comforter so that I don't easily fall over. While my muscles still ache, the soreness has lessened. Maybe

Justine going on and on about heat therapy wasn't as crazy as she sounded.

With caution, I make my way out of the bedroom in time to see Luca walking through the front door, holding a silver tray of food.

The smile he sends my way nearly puts me on my ass, and I have to grab the couch to keep myself upright.

He sets the tray on the coffee table, which has been restored to its rightful place now that the medical equipment is gone. He's by my side in an instant. "Are you okay? You shouldn't be out of bed."

"How would you know?" I ask teasingly. "You sent the doctor away."

"And I can bring him back just as quickly," he grumbles in my ear before grabbing my chin and pressing his lips to mine.

I gasp from the unexpected contact. Kissing him is like feeling the warm sun on my skin, heating my soul. Damn, if I don't need more.

My fingers grab on to his shirt and hold him close. "I thought you were gone."

"You've been asleep for over twelve hours," he says, then nods toward the food. "I was just getting breakfast so I could wake you up with something other than bad news."

An emotional lump forms in my throat, and tears threaten my eyes. "Tori? She's not..."

"No," he says quickly. "At least, not according to the information we have. But I still don't have her back."

I release the pent-up breath and move to sit on the new black leather couch. According to Justine, the other was ruined by Luca's blood.

"But you will," I finally reply, though I'm not sure if those words are more for me or him.

"We know where she is, so yes, it's likely we will." He speaks the words so casually that I almost don't register that he's said he knows where she is.

"Wait a second." I turn my head toward him, my glare sharp. "If you know where she is, why hasn't she been rescued from Titan?"

"Because it's not safe," he retorts, his tone matching my intensity. "I could go in shooting everyone in my way, but that's the fastest way to get her killed. Right now, she's safe."

"What does that even mean?" It's not my intention to be angry with him, but I know that's the way it's coming out, especially when he's acting as if this isn't a huge deal. Just yesterday, I could have sworn that his fury matched my own. Not that I assume Luca gives a shit about Tori, but he at least seems to care enough about me to want her alive.

He bends to a knee in front of me, grabbing both of my cheeks until he has my full attention. "Listen to me, Raven. I know I didn't say this yesterday when we got the news. Though, I assumed it was implied. I promise to do everything in my power to get your friend back, but you need to trust me. Can you do that?"

I exhale harshly. "Of course."

"Good." His hands move from my face to my thighs, lightly squeezing them both. "Now, eat your breakfast so I can have mine."

I blink several times, my brain again not processing his words. At least, not as fast as the rest of my body does. My breath comes in soft pants, and there's an ache between my legs that I haven't felt in days.

Luca grips my chin and forces my mouth open before feeding me a piece of bacon. "Eat, Olivia."

"Yes, Sir," I murmur between frantic bites.

When his eyes darken, I swear the world falls out from under me.

"Faster," he commands, then rises from his kneeling position.

I don't waste any time, reaching for the only plate on the tray. It's filled with eggs, bacon, sausage, and a bowl of mixed fruit. "Where are you going?" I ask before shoveling random bits of food into my mouth.

When he turns back toward me, the hunger in his eyes nearly undoes me. "I'm getting naked, Raven."

And I'm officially dead.

With no offense to Luca, sex had been the last thing on my mind when I first woke up, but as much as I love Tori and need to have her out of Titan's hands... If I'm not feeling like death at the moment and Luca isn't stressed about my missing best friend after what he's learned, then I'm going to do my best not to be either, because fuck me. I can't wait a moment longer to have this man again.

Within record time, my plate is cleared except for the fruit, which I intend to consume later. Still being careful not to push myself too far, I stand slowly from the couch, then strip off my tank top and sleep shorts I'd changed into the night before.

Just as I assumed, it's a struggle to get my clothes off without wincing, but that's exactly why I get undressed in the living room. I don't need Luca changing his mind about having his way with me. Not after saying I'm his breakfast.

My pussy needs him too damn much.

Once I'm naked and walking toward the bedroom, I realize maybe I should have stayed dressed. The bruises covering my body aren't exactly sexy, but there's nothing I can do about them. It's not as if he wasn't going to see them anyway. It's mid-morning. The house isn't dark, and he isn't stupid.

I push the worries aside and stride into the bedroom, fixing my gaze on Luca's as soon as I step through the doorway.

Just as he said, he's naked and waiting for me on my side of the bed. His dark eyes roam over my body, and instead of the disgust I thought I might see on his face from my injuries, I only see an insatiable hunger in his stare.

He closes the distance between us, stopping in front of me, and hovering his hands around my shoulders before moving them down my arms and over my hips. His skin never grazes mine, but the heat from his palms burns into me, lighting every part of my body on fire.

I close my eyes as my head tilts back, giving my body over to him. His lips move over my neck, and his breath sears every inch that it reaches as he moves south.

"Luca," I beg. Though, I'm not sure exactly what for.

When I feel his mouth on my ribs, I open my eyes to find him on his knees in front of me, kissing every bruise and cut on my body. "I will break a bone in his body for all fifty-three bruises on yours."

"You counted?" I ask, surprised and having no clue when he did that, but also loving that he had.

"If you haven't learned yet, I like to be precise."

Oh, I have. He also likes to be in control, and I'm more than happy to let him take the lead with me.

As his kisses lead further down my stomach, I don't even realize I've spread my shaking legs until he slides his fingers over my pussy and hums in approval. "I wasn't sure you'd be ready." He puts both fingers into his mouth, keeping his eyes on me as he tastes my arousal. "Get on the bed, Raven."

Without needing to be told twice, I move forward, but stop when I remember it's not exactly easy for me to climb onto the tall bed just yet. Though, I'm not standing there long.

Luca is behind me and cradles my body into his arms before leaning over as far as he can on the mattress and placing me near the middle. "Arms up and legs spread."

His demand sends a delicious shiver through my

body and has me wanting to touch myself, but I don't dare defy him. Not when I need him more than I ever have before.

My eyes watch him move around to the foot of the bed. As he crawls over the comforter, my eyes are glued to his hard cock pointed in my direction.

I start to move my arm down and reach for him, but he backs off, voice deepening. "I said arms up."

He's in a mood, and I'm not at all mad about it.

Doing as he says, I can't stop from smiling, but my grin swiftly turns into an "O" when he glides his tongue over my pussy, then sucks on my clit.

My hips surge upward, a motion that hurts, but the pain doesn't outweigh the euphoria of being devoured by this powerful man.

Luca's arm pins me down as he continues to lap at me, his eyes never leaving mine. I can't tear my stare away from him. His mouth consumes me like I'm a delicacy he's been waiting for his whole life.

The muscles in my stomach tighten with ripples of pleasure that move from lower in my belly, down my legs, and up both arms, forcing my fingers to curl and grip the pillow behind me. It's killing me not to reach for him, but I'm afraid if I do, he'll stop. The thought of that is even worse. My breathing becomes more ragged, and I can't stop my thighs from tightening around his head.

Luca seems to understand that I'm close to coming, because he adds a finger to his movements, then another, pulsing them in and out of me as he sucks on my clit once again.

My back arches off the bed, sending my chest into the air and my head tilting backward. My moans get louder, and I can't hold anything back. I don't want to, either.

"Fuck, Luca," I hiss between my teeth, everything inside my body coiling tightly in preparation for the explosion I know is about to happen.

"Come for me, Raven," he whispers over my pussy, sending a vibration from his words through the rest of me. "Now."

And I do. The command pushes me over the edge, and my eyes squeeze so tightly together that I see stars. I cry out his name over and over again, equal parts wishing he would stop devouring me and hoping he never stops.

I can hardly breathe, and when I open my eyes, Luca's are still on mine. There's a lightness in them I haven't seen since returning, which has me smiling once more.

"How are you feeling?" he asks, his hands running up and down my trembling thighs.

With a groan I say, "Like I might never leave this bed."

"I'd rather enjoy that." He moves like a predator over me. "But how is your body feeling?"

The lie falls easily from my lips. "Like a million bucks. Completely healed. Now, fuck me with your cock like you just did with your mouth."

He shakes his head. "I should tell you no just for lying to me."

"But you won't." I reach between us, finally wrapping my fingers around his dick and stroking him. "You need me just as much as I need you."

He brushes a few strands of hair away from my eyes and says, "Possibly even more."

If a human heart could burst, I'm certain mine would right now. This deadly, dangerous, and striking man *needs* me. His acknowledgment of that takes my breath away, and when he kisses me next, I swear I've died and gone to heaven.

His tongue pushes between my lips, and I taste not only him but myself as he deepens the kiss, owning my mouth just like he does the rest of me.

My hold on his cock increases as I guide him toward my waiting pussy. When he starts to sink inside me oh-so-slowly while still owning my mouth, I know right then and there that I never want to be apart from this man again.

No matter the risks, Luca Monroe is all *mine*.

15

LUCA

Fully seated within Olivia, ready to remind her body who it belongs to, I still can't stop thinking she deserves better than this life. She's more kind than she should be, patient when I'm being obstinate, and doesn't judge me—at least most of the time.

But in moments like this, when it's just the two of us and I get to fuck her like this, I can let the rest of the world fade away, ignoring all the reasons I should let her go.

As I start to move above her, I try to avoid letting my eyes linger too long on her bruises, reminders that she should still be resting. I should wait longer to ravage her, but I can't resist any longer. Not when I think we both need the pleasure to replace all the pain.

I rest on one elbow while my other hand glides up her thigh, over her hip, and across her stomach. I grip her full breast between my fingers, pinching until her nipple pebbles to my satisfaction.

Her eyes are on mine as I stare down at her, and the admiration that I see in her gaze nearly has me looking away, but I don't. I hold on to the care she's showing me and use it to battle my past. To not push her away. To believe that nothing, and no one, will ever be able to tear us apart.

"Luca," she purrs, pushing her head further back and exposing her neck.

I seize the opportunity to nip along her jawline, moving further down and along her collarbone as my hips start to move faster.

Even with Olivia's beauty as a distraction, I'm still mindful of her injuries. I don't slam into her like I crave, but instead, keep a steady pace that she seems to have no problems meeting.

My eyes stay on her face, watching for any signs of pain, but all I see is pleasure within her bright blue eyes, flushed cheeks, and relaxed, sexy mouth. A mouth I hope to have around my cock very fucking soon.

Her nails dig into my arms as she writhes beneath me. "More."

"I don't want to hurt you, Raven," I murmur against her neck, keeping my body close to hers.

She places her hands on both sides of my face and forces my head back. "Don't treat me differently, Luca. I'm not glass. I've been through hell, and there are cracks in my exterior, but I didn't shatter. I need this. I need *you*."

Damn her.

"I don't want to hurt you," I practically growl, repeating myself. Though, I already notice my speed getting faster, forcing me to accept that even my body can't deny her.

"You won't," she says sternly. "I promise."

Instead of risking her recovery by fully unleashing my desire on her, I pull out and lay on my back and guide her gently over me. "Then, take whatever you need."

I expect her to guide my cock toward her pussy, but she surprises me when she moves to kneel between my legs. Her hand grips the base before pulling up just rough enough.

A saucy grin lifts on her face. "I think I will."

When I said I wanted her mouth on my dick soon, I didn't think today would be that day. I nearly stop her, but the moment her lips wrap around the head, there's no stopping her.

She opens her mouth wide, taking me deeper as her hand continues to stroke the lower half. When her tongue swirls around the sensitive skin, my body instinctively reacts, pushing my hips forward and putting the head at the back of her throat.

The strangled sound she makes has tingles expanding through my balls. I fist a handful of her hair, momentarily forgetting her injuries, and try to jerk her back before she makes me come too soon, but the vixen fights me.

Her glorious mouth sucks harder, and I end up pushing her back down, choking her until there are tears leaking from the corners of her eyes. Even still, she licks and pulls at my cock with fervor, taking me deeper with every thrust.

And I didn't think she could be any more perfect...

Finally, I have to draw her up, because I'll be damned if I finish without her pussy tightening around me. This time, she doesn't fight me, and as she wipes at the side of her mouth, her grin returns.

Neither of us says anything as she mounts me. Before she can slide too slowly onto my dick, I surge up, hard and fast, eliciting the gasp from her that I so desperately want to hear.

Olivia's hands slap over my chest, and her nails dig into my skin as she tilts her hips back, taking every inch of me as if we were made for each other.

I grip her sides, guiding her, but there's little need for me to do so. She rides my cock with abandon, her head tilted back, silky black hair dangling around her, and her chest heaving in time with our movements.

Her tits bounce in front of me, and since she doesn't need much assistance from me, I reach up to pinch both nipples between my fingers and smirk as her pussy flexes.

"So close," she mutters from above, and I start to surge my hips up. With my hands back on her waist, she slams down harder on my dick, each moan growing louder by the second.

The shiver that runs along my spine goes straight to my tightening balls, and I know I'm not far behind her. She fucks me without a care in the world. As if everything around us hasn't been falling apart. Right then, as her entire body tenses before exploding around me, I know.

Olivia Danes is all I will ever need in this world. The mafia, the business, all of it can fuck right off as long as I have her.

The trust she has in me is my undoing.

My cock twitches inside her pulsing pussy, filling her with my cum, and I wrap my arms around her when she leans forward, laying on top of me.

She turns her head towards me, peppering light kisses along my neck. "That was..."

"If you say 'pleasant,' I will smack your ass until it welts," I warn, a playful glint in my eyes, before she can complete her sentence.

Her responding chuckle vibrates through my body. "Magnificent. Though, I'm already wishing you had a tub to soak in."

"I'll have the bathroom remodeled this week." A bathtub never held an appeal for me, but if my Raven wants one, then she'll have the best.

She pushes up to stare at me. "You can't simply snap your fingers and have a bathroom remodeled."

"Can't I?" I raise an eyebrow, a smirk tugging at my lips. "You're dating the leader of a mafia family now. I can and will have whatever I damn well please."

"Just how rich are you?" Her question is cautious, as if she's unsure whether she should ask.

"Enough that I don't ask how much something is when I want it," I answer, moving my palms over her back.

"Must be nice not to have to worry about bills," she muses and starts to roll over, wincing as she goes, so I don't fight her.

I shift onto my side and face her, needing to know if this is going to be a problem. "And neither do you. I paid every bill attached to your mother's house."

She tenses, but not for long. Instead, there's a longing in her face that I don't expect.

"Tori and I were supposed to go through everything at the house together when I was ready," she says softly. "What if I don't get that chance?"

"You will. I promise," I say. "We know where Tori is, and from what we've seen, she doesn't even realize she's being held captive. At least, not that she's showing."

This has Olivia's attention back on me. "What do you mean?"

"We went to the last house that Titan owns," I tell her since I didn't get to last night. "She was sitting in the living room, watching TV with a bowl of popcorn in her lap."

I anticipate relief, so when her eyes well up with tears, and she turns away from me, I'm taken aback.

Gently, I grasp her chin and redirect her gaze towards me. "What's wrong?"

"I'm a horrible person," she mumbles, struggling to meet my gaze.

"You couldn't be, even if you tried," I reply. "Tell me what's upsetting you."

Her lip quivers until she takes a deep breath, regaining control of her emotions. "He didn't hurt her."

And suddenly her tears make sense. Titan didn't hurt Tori, someone not of his blood, but he had no problem beating the fuck out of his only child.

With the utmost care, I pull her into my arms and hold her close. "And he'll pay for that too, Raven. For everything."

She nods against my chest, and I want to say something else, but the fury within me is all-consuming. How could that bastard not look at Olivia and see perfection? How could he raise a single finger toward her or allow anyone else to without feeling this...unrelenting wrath?

Titan Moretti has a lot to pay for, but hurting Olivia is the one transgression I won't let myself forget when I finally have him within my grasp.

16

OLIVIA

Another day passes, and while I'm told I don't need to worry about Tori, I still do. There is so much fury storming within me that I can't stop thinking about her or the piece of shit that took her.

Luca, along with Justine, have both insisted that Titan is nothing and that I deserved a better father, but these words alone can't silence my mind. This might be exactly what he wants—for me to fret over Tori. Clearly, she isn't being hidden; Titan wants me to know he's got her under his control, making her think he's shielding her from the big, bad mafia man named Luca Monroe.

If only she knew the real story. If only I'd been honest with her.

Luca is already out of the apartment this morning. I promised him I was fine, but as I climb out of bed, I know that being with him yesterday set me back. Though, I have no regrets. Luca's presence stitches up the emotional wounds more effectively than any medicine, and right now, those wounds run deeper than the physical ones.

The upside is that Justine's cream is working its magic; my bruises have already transitioned to a garish green-yellow hue. However, my rib still throbs in protest.

Dr. Theo came by last night and gave me some anti-inflammatory meds to help with the pain since the painkillers he left before were making me nauseous. As long as I don't move too fast or try to bend, then I can stay...moderately comfortable. That's what I try to portray to everyone else around me, at least.

I take a shower, which lasts longer than normal since raising my arms above my head also hurts, but I manage to get washed all by myself. When I'm done, I nearly yelp at Justine waltzing into the bedroom dressed in jeans and a dirtied white shirt with a hardhat under her arm and a clipboard in hand.

"What the hell are you doing in my room dressed like that?" I ask more accusingly than I intend to.

She smirks and raises a brow. "*Your* room, huh? I mean, when Luca asked me to include a bathroom remodel with all the other renovations this morning, I assumed, but good to have a confirmation."

Her eyebrows waggle at me, and I shake my head. "You are ridiculous."

"I most certainly am, but only in the best ways." She chuckles, and I know if I reply, it will only encourage her. "So, that bathroom remodel. I need to take some measurements, then you'll be able to pick out the tub you want, assuming Luca isn't the one wanting a good, long soak."

"I hate you," I murmur with my back to her as I hang my towel on the corner of my dresser and start to get dressed. Though, when I open my dresser drawer, none of my clothes are in there.

"Something missing?" Justine asks with amusement. "Or do you prefer to air dry?"

Carefully, I grab my towel and cover myself back up before turning around and heading toward the closet. I assume after everything Luca has done that he wouldn't have thrown all of my things out. Maybe he just made some room for me within the closet. The longer I think about that, the more shocked I am. He's slowly becoming someone I didn't believe him to be capable of when he first locked me up in his basement.

Sure enough, when I open up the doors to the walk-in closet, the few clothes that had been brought here for me—plus several more outfits—have been hung up, only half-filling the one side that's been cleared out.

Justine makes me jump when she murmurs in my ear. "New tub, space in the closet, and new clothes... Yeah, I'd say things are getting serious."

Instead of fighting against her cockiness and excitement, I return her grin and nod. "I think I have to agree."

"Of course, you do," she says, following me. "I can't

wait to take you shopping. We'll need two cars. One to hold all our shit and another to drive us around."

Her laughter has me shaking my head, but mostly because I know she's absolutely serious. Although, nothing of the sort will be happening until we have Tori and she knows the truth.

I freeze as I reach for a t-shirt. "Sandi."

"No, that would be more cream-colored than sandy," Justine says, seeming to think I'm talking about the shirt in my hand.

I shake my head. "My old co-worker. Sandi. She checked on me before. Hell, she's the reason I was even in the auction where I first saw Luca. I texted her back a couple times when I had my phone, but what if Titan takes her, too? He has my phone. He could have gotten into it, looked through my shit."

Just because the psycho isn't hurting Tori, doesn't mean he wouldn't do anything rash to Sandi.

"Well, it's a good thing that Jaxon was tasked with getting you a new phone when he left this morning," she says reassuringly, then adds. "He should be back within the hour."

Thank fuck, because until I can reach her, I'm going to be stressed the hell out.

Justine heads to the bathroom to finish her task of measuring for my new tub, and I grin at how much she seems to be enjoying her new role of foreman for all the remodeling.

Once I'm dressed, I head into the bathroom to do my

hair. She's taking pictures, a serious expression on her face as she concentrates.

When she notices me staring, she doesn't stop her task, but says, "I haven't had real purpose since I moved in here. I've had to earn Luca's trust, which I can respect, but still. Until you showed up, I was bored out of my damn mind. A girl can only do so much shopping. This job is still a bit like that, but so much better because I get to tell people what to do."

I can see the appeal, and I'm more than happy for her. Plus, it's better her than me. I have zero desire to be in charge of a construction project. Though, if Luca really does have all this money to throw around, I just might have to take advantage and do a few good deeds once all the craziness dies down.

"Want to come downstairs with me and have lunch?" Justine asks when she finishes making her notes.

I don't know why, but I tense. I've never eaten outside of the apartment. Hell, I've hardly been around the house unless I was sneaking around. This has been my space. My safe space.

"You don't have to if you're not feeling up to it," she adds when I don't reply.

"It's not that..." I fumble for an explanation, but the truth is, I don't have a valid reason to object.

She gestures to my face. "You can barely even see the bruises on your cheeks, and the cut on your forehead is covered by your hair. And even if that wasn't the case, nobody would judge you. Shit, they probably won't even make eye contact with you, knowing you're Luca's woman."

I muster a smile to my face just for her and ignore any unfounded reservations. "I'd love to have lunch with you downstairs."

She leans in close. "You're so full of shit, but I'm not letting you back out now. I'm going to get out of my work clothes and be back up here in five. You better be ready."

This is one of those moments that I equally love and hate her.

I stay in the bathroom and braid my hair since blow-drying it would take more effort than I have to give but letting it air dry would lead to frizzy hair. By the time I'm done and get my shoes on, Justine is back, wearing a stunning green dress that makes her eyes and hair pop in the best way.

"Don't you look gorgeous," I say with a warm smile.

She gives me a little twirl. "It's our first official friend date. I had to dress up."

My eyes cast down at my jeans, white Vans, and plain cream-colored shirt. "I should change."

"Absolutely not." She grabs my hand but doesn't tug too hard. "You're perfect as you are. Come on. I smelled fries earlier, and my mouth hasn't stopped watering since."

I move to follow her, but she stops abruptly, turning back around. "Oh. I have your new phone. Jaxon was in the room when I got there."

She hands me the already-charged device and I

quickly open it, thankful I have nearly everything backed up on a cloud. All I have to do is log in and wait for the phone to sync.

Once I've done what I can, Justine and I head for the elevator. I manage to only check the phone's progress twice on the way down, eager to contact Sandi.

We step into the hallway on the first floor, and I glance around. Tarps are up, blocking off certain areas where I assume they're doing repairs, but the way to the kitchen is clear. As we get nearer, I start to smell the food and my stomach grumbles until it begins to ache.

I guess I shouldn't have slept through breakfast.

"Oh, French Dip." Justine moans. "My favorite."

As good as everything smells and hungry as I am, my phone finally loads all of my contacts and I immediately find a seat at the counter as I scroll to Sandi's number, then realize I don't even know what day of the week it is. I back out of the address book and check the calendar. It's Saturday. She's not going to be at work, so hopefully she answers.

I click on her name and press her phone number. My teeth scrape against my lower lip, and the tip of my foot taps on the ground as I wait for her answer.

Just when I think she's not going to, I finally hear, "Hey, Stranger."

"Hey, yourself," I say, trying to act calmer than I feel. "What are you up to?"

"Oh, just wondering where you're at and how

worried I should be that you basically disappeared off the face of the Earth after that auction."

There's something off about her tone, and my chest begins to tighten.

"Listen, Sandi," I plead. "I can't tell you much. I just need you to know that I'm safe and if anyone tries to tell you otherwise, scream and run in the opposite direction."

She hums, and I wish I could see her face right now. "And why should I do that?"

"Because...I just need you to trust me," I implore. "There's been some stuff going on, and I don't know how far the consequences will reach. I just need to know that you'll be careful and stay safe."

"So, this handsome man standing in front of me, dressed in a suit and smelling like a million bucks, I should run and scream from him?"

As the words leave her mouth, I swear I'm seconds from passing out. "Sandi, I'm so sorry. Just run from wherever you are."

My heart is pounding, and my eyes burn with unshed tears. What the fuck have I done?

"Raven, she's perfectly safe."

The sound of Luca's voice has my head snapping up, but he's not here in this house. No, the words echoed from Sandi's side of the call.

"Luca is with you?" I ask, shocked to my core. He continues to surprise me with everything he does. Especially when I'm sure he never would have mentioned that he took it upon himself to check on my friend just like he hadn't when he paid all of my bills.

Sandi falls silent for a beat. "At least that's what he said his name is. I take it he's the reason you've been MIA?"

I still can't breathe right, but at least my panic is settling. "Sort of. I don't know what he's told you—"

"Pretty much the same thing you just did," she cuts in. "Which makes his story more believable. Though, I don't like that you're in danger because I roped you into that auction."

I want to laugh and cry at that. "Honestly, I think it would have found me one way or another. Just know that Luca is making sure I'm okay."

"Uh huh. I bet he is." She chuckles, and that finally has a smile gracing my face as I rest my forearms on the counter. "I expect dinner and drinks when whatever this has passed. And don't let this one go. He's hot."

"And you're married, so quit ogling." I shake my head as I say the words, but I'm also thankful that she isn't making this into a big deal. While it is one, not having to over-explain or lie is appreciated more than she may ever know.

"My vows didn't include not being able to appreciate other men," she retorts, and I can hear the grin on her face. "I just can't touch and I'm okay with that. You can keep him all to yourself."

"You're incredible," is all I can think of to reply with.

"I know. But hey, I need to go. I was just leaving my

house when he showed up," she says. "Don't wait so long to call again. Work is dreadful without you there."

"I'm sure." I laugh, my cheeks aching. "And I'll stay in touch, I promise."

As I hang up, the pressure on my chest lightens. Although the weight of the world still rests there, it's not as crushing as it was earlier. And while I'm thankful Sandi took everything so well, I'm more grateful to Luca.

Who knew falling for your kidnapper could be so damned easy?

17

LUCA

I take the liberty of not only finding Sandi, but also checking on Tori again. I wasn't looking forward to the former, but the woman handled everything with ease, almost as if she didn't truly believe there was a danger to her life.

If that's what she needs to believe to sleep better at night, then I won't be the one to force her to think otherwise. I did what needed to be done and then some when I left one of my men to keep an eye on her from a distance.

The last thing we need right now is for Titan to get a hold of someone else Olivia cares about.

Driving across town, I arrive down the street from where Tori is being kept. The house next to me is modest, but big enough to fit into this neighborhood of mini mansions. An idea crosses my mind that may help our situation, depending on how long we're here, but it's something I'll need to follow up on later.

Markus is waiting, having been put on watch today to make sure she doesn't get moved or disappear from our sight for too long.

Getting out of the vehicle, I make the walk toward the SUV he's camped out in and slide into the back with him as swiftly as possible.

My thigh—where the bullet wound is still healing—isn't thrilled each time I sit down and put pressure on it, but with my activity lessened now that Olivia is back, I haven't had to take any extra meds.

"Anything to report?" I ask him.

He turns toward me, his dark eyes meeting my stare and his face otherwise expressionless. "The girl did yoga this morning. Damon stayed to watch. Two more men arrived around nine and none have left since then."

"How many total does that make in the house?" I stare at the two-story home with its brick siding and white shutter windows. The yard is pristine with freshly cut grass and varying colors of rose bushes around the edges.

Markus runs a hand through his longer brunet hair. "Unless we've missed someone, fourteen including the girl."

I don't miss that he's called her "the girl" twice now. I know it's his way of disassociating from the situation, and I don't blame him, either, but he's the most elusive of our crew. After Vin's betrayal, I decided I need to make an effort to draw him out more. Allowing him to remain withdrawn doesn't seem like the best idea any longer.

Using my phone, I take a picture of Tori when I see her back in the living room. She's playing cards by herself and seems perfectly content.

"Do you need anything?" I ask, knowing that there isn't a reason for both of us to be here.

He shakes his head, but then points at the house. "Titan."

My attention goes back to the open windows. Titan stands next to Tori. He's dressed in khakis and a white polo. He seems to also be growing out a beard, or at least some stubble, likely to hide the scars on his face.

He smiles down at Tori who looks up at him with nothing other than admiration and trust.

When he pats the top of her head with affection, I want to storm into the house and put a bullet in his head, but I refrain.

We made the decision to wait for multiple reasons, and I intend to honor that. The most important being that if we storm in there, I have no doubt Tori will either be killed on site or she'll be promptly taken away, possibly never to be found again.

Secondly, I want to know what Titan is up to. Why is he doing this? Why fuck with me and my business when his has been doing just fine? Olivia can't be the reason since the senator was killed before I technically met her. So, there's something else that I'm missing, and I want to know what.

If that information dies with Titan, there's no telling if some other idiot is going to attempt to carry out whatever this is.

"I saw Bryson earlier," Markus says, which is news to me. I would have preferred he told me that as soon as I arrived.

"What was he doing?" I ask, also remembering the unknown person he seems to deem worthy of protection.

Markus continues to watch the house as he speaks. "Walking past the dining room. Seemed to be in one piece from what I could see."

"Was he alone?" I ask and Markus nods before I add, "If you see him with anyone, I want photos."

"Sure."

Markus's clipped reply grates on my nerves, and I can't stop from saying something. "You know, if you don't want to be here anymore, you just have to say so."

"By here, I don't assume you mean in this SUV watching a girl that means nothing to us," he confirms. When I don't reply, he continues. "You chose me because I held no attachments. Are you wanting that to change?"

He's right. When we met fifteen years ago, I knew he would be a solid addition to the team, but knowing that I can't be too careful any longer, I don't back down from the conversation now that it's been started.

"You don't need to change, but you need to be honest," I say. "I don't need people around who don't want to be here. Minds change, and I want to make sure yours hasn't."

A deep line forms between his eyes. "I'm not Vin."

"And I'm not saying you are," I reply earnestly. "But this is still my family. I want you to stay a part of that, but don't feel like you're being forced to. You can't tell me that you haven't withdrawn over the last couple years, more so in the last six months."

Bringing Justine into the house hadn't helped Markus's mood. I know that even if he'd never admit it, and I know that Olivia will be a cause of discontent, but I won't tolerate it in the least.

He moves to watch the house again. "I'm fine, Luca. You don't need to worry about me."

My hand grasps the top of his shoulder. "You're family. The most important thing to me. Not worrying is impossible."

He says nothing in return and doesn't remove his stare from the house. I'm not surprised, but I'm also glad I said something. If anything, the conversation will give him something to think about while he's here alone.

Not that I want to lose him, but if he's going to continue to withdraw, then maybe this isn't the place for him any longer. Yes, I consider him family, but there are others I need to protect within that family as well. I intend on doing so until my dying breath.

I leave the SUV and head back to my car. When I get in, I check my phone and there's a text from Olivia.

Olivia: You could have told me what you were doing today. Thank you.

Me: I don't do what I do for your thanks.

Olivia: And that's one of the reasons I haven't run away screaming.

As I drive back to the house, I can't help wondering once again if I should push her away. It's not what I want, but she should have run from me the moment she had the chance. She hadn't, and while I want to consider that a good thing—that she was meant to be in this world—I also know she deserves better than the fucked-up life I live.

By the time I get back to the compound, I'm decided in my choice to keep Olivia close. Selfish or not, right or not, I won't second guess my decision. Not again. She's mine, and I'll keep her safe every day moving forward. I won't let her be hurt a third time on my watch. Not even over my dead body.

I head straight to the kitchen, having skipped breakfast since Olivia was sleeping and knowing that lunch should be out still. The house cook Alina has been working for me over a year, and she's heeded every one of my rules with the utmost respect.

The kitchen is always spotless, along with the common areas on the first floor. Food is always prepared on time, and we are never out of anything deemed a necessity within the house. She even takes anything not eaten by the following day's end to the homeless center, sharing with those who might go without otherwise.

It's not as if our family struggled growing up, but hunger is a trigger for me that I don't admit to anyone. My father used to use it as a punishment when I didn't do what he wanted or say the right thing. Even as a young child, he had no problem locking me in my room for entire days without food or the use of a bathroom.

Those memories don't often come to my mind, and as soon as I walk in the kitchen to find Olivia and Justine there, it's easily dashed away, replaced by thoughts of how fucking stunning my Raven is.

She's laughing with Justine, and I realize I don't see her do that often enough. She has an empty plate in front of her. When she was locked away by Titan, the bastard didn't feed her, and the evidence of that treatment was clear when I brought her back.

Seeing her here and knowing her appetite is coming back is a relief I didn't realize I needed.

Ignoring the tempting aroma of food, I walk over to her and wrap a hand around the back of her neck before pressing my mouth to hers.

Now that I've kissed her, I don't know that I'll ever be able to stop. She tastes of things I haven't allowed myself to hope for in much too long, and I don't want to let go now that I have her.

She kisses me back with matching need, but the action is cut short when Justine whistles. "I guess our friend date has come to an end."

Olivia pulls back and grabs her arm before she can leave. "Absolutely not. We're going to the garden as planned."

I want to keep her to myself, but I won't be selfish enough to ruin her plans. Plus, I still have things to do for work that I've been neglecting, so I nod. "Have your fun.

I just needed that before I grab food and head to my office."

"The one here or at work?" Olivia asks with a glint in her eyes.

"Here." I answer, hoping that means I'll see her there before I'm done.

Justine grabs her hand. "Come on, my little nympho friend. I'm getting you out of here before I lose you completely."

I kiss Olivia once more, and when she's pulled from my arms, I do my best not to glare at Justine. She's only doing what Olivia needs, and even in the moments I hate having her away from me, I want her to be happy here. That means I can't be the only reason she stays.

No matter how much I wish otherwise.

18

OLIVIA

After being in the garden for nearly two hours with Justine, our friend date has concluded. As hesitant as I'd been to leave the apartment, I'm more grateful than ever that she got me out of there. I'm still not sure what I was afraid of—maybe just the idea of being taken again—but now that I've ventured out, I don't have any desire to go back to the empty apartment.

Saying goodbye to Justine with promises to see her again tomorrow for breakfast or lunch, depending on how things are looking with Tori, I head to Luca's office in hopes that he has positive updates for me.

I let yesterday go by without pressuring him for more information after he reassured me that Tori was safe. More than that, I didn't want to think any more about how Titan hadn't laid a finger on her.

Do I feel like a terrible person for those thoughts? Absolutely, but more than that, I'm glad she's safe. Deep down, I know the guilt of having my best friend hurt because of me would be far worse than being jealous that she's being treated with respect.

When I step into the elevator, I take another look at the painting I did while Justine had her fun planning for more than flowers on the balcony and talking about getting a greenhouse for year-round, home-grown vegetables. I didn't expect it from her, but I have a feeling that making this "compound" more of a home now that we're both here is going to be something she succeeds at, no matter how long it takes.

And I'm going to have no problem helping her. Though, the idea of living here and not at my mother's house as previously planned does cause an ache in my chest, especially as I take in my latest painting.

It's the first time I've created anything since being kidnapped by Titan. The colors are darker than normal. More deep blues and purples with forest green foliage added between the violets. It's good and something I intend to give Luca, but it's different.

Then again, so am I. I'm not the same woman I was a month ago. Hell, not even last week. I thought that would frighten me, but I'm choosing to embrace these changes as I realize I'm stronger than I thought possible. More than that, though, I know I don't have to do any of this alone.

I lost my mother, my only blood family that I've been close to throughout my life, and Tori is... Well, I don't want to think too hard about that right now. Regardless, I have a new sense of peace and belonging because of the people here. Mafia life be damned, I can see myself making a new family here and not feeling so fucking alone.

When Mom died unexpectedly, I knew I still had Tori and even Sandi on a certain level, but I think a lot of my numbness came from knowing that my circle was just that much smaller. Now it's not, and that knowledge is what's kept me moving forward instead of wallowing in the trauma of all that's transpired.

I arrive at Luca's office back on the first floor, and I'm glad his door is open because I wasn't entirely sure I would remember which room was his. I felt pretty confident in the general vicinity, but I was mostly guessing once I turned down the hallway, allowing my thoughts to keep me distracted.

As I step inside, his eyes are focused on the computer and fingers are flying over the keyboard with a precision I don't expect from him. Though, he's confident in everything he does, even this work. I shouldn't have expected anything less.

When I sit down in the chair, still holding my painting in front of me, I remain quiet, not wanting to interrupt whatever he's working on. But it's only a second later that his eyes shift toward me, even while his fingers keep typing away.

"What do you have there, Raven?" he asks, glancing down at the canvas in my lap.

"Just a little something I painted while I was with

Justine." I keep the art turned away from him until he's done typing and use that time to glance around his office.

It has an industrial feel to it with exposed brick, metal piping, and tarnished yet pristine wood furnishing. There are shelves on one side of the room, filled with books and a few keepsakes I intend to get a better look at, but as soon as my eyes move to the other side of the room, I forget about everything else.

Hanging on the opposite wall, front and center, is the painting of my ass and boobs, now framed with a chestnut wood that matches his desk and shelves. My eyes widen, but at the same time, a smile forms on my face. I take in the mess that is my personal body parts and think back to how perfect that day was before we left the garden.

There had been so much joy in there. A peace had settled within me and had me feeling confident about my choice to stay with Luca. But within the blink of an eye, my world had been turned upside down.

"What do you think?" he asks, catching me by surprise since I didn't realize he had finished typing.

"I think I'm shocked you have that painting on your wall." I chuckle, trying to hide the tension that's begun to rise within me.

He stands and comes around his desk, stopping once he's in front of me. "I had it framed the day after you were taken, then hung it in my office, so I could enjoy the view in here for once."

My smile turns into a smirk. "And you don't care that

anyone who comes in here will get a view of my...ass and boob prints?"

Given how possessive he's shown me he can be, I'm a little surprised the painting isn't hidden behind something. Though, I also love that it's out for anyone to see. As if he's proud of the creation he made using my body as his paintbrush.

"The only person who might risk commenting on it would be Jaxon," he says with his own grin. "I have that effect on people."

"Not all people," I counter, rising to my feet and setting the new painting on his desk before placing my palms on his chest.

His forehead presses against mine as he moves closer. "Yes, you seem to be immune to the fear I typically instill in others."

"If you only knew how truly afraid I was of you in those first few days," I reply, my voice soft.

"Afraid?" Both of his brows raise. "You made a wall of pillows on my bed. I had the impression you were more revolted by me than anything else."

"We both know that's not true." I chuckle, curling my fingers around the edges of his opened suitcoat. "Stupidly, I wanted you the moment we were alone in that SUV."

He presses his lips to mine in a quick kiss. "I don't think there's anything *stupid* about that."

"Of course, you wouldn't." My head shakes, and I

move to kiss him again, but he reaches for the painting I've left turned over on his desk.

"What's this?" he asks, running his hand lightly over the dried acrylic.

I glance down at the violets. "I was going to give it to you, but seeing as you already have a painting in here, maybe I'll bring it back to the apartment."

He snatches the art and moves away from me to place it behind his desk. "Or I'll keep it and have it framed to hang next to the other."

That works for me and makes my chest expand with a warmth I haven't felt in...maybe ever. None of my past relationships have made me feel as Luca does. From the moment I met him, there's been this exhilaration inside me just by being in his presence.

Even through the initial fear, there was an underlying draw and curiosity that I couldn't ignore, nor did I want to. His commanding presence drew me in, a part of me wondering what it would feel like to be commanded by him.

For so long, I've had to be responsible for not only my own life, but for checking in on my mother, making sure she wasn't too lonely, working my ass off to survive living on my own, trying to make my dream of running my own business come true.

Not having to take care of all the things makes me grateful to Luca for taking care of my needs, even when I initially was upset with him for doing so. Understanding myself better now, I was merely afraid that by him paying my debts I would owe him more than I could repay.

Except that's not who Luca is. He does things because he wants to. Not because of what he might gain from doing them. I'm sure that's not the case with all of his business transactions, but I'm confident that's the truth here.

As soon as he sets the painting down, he goes to the door and closes it before turning back to me. "How are you feeling today?"

I'm sore as shit, but I can't tell him that. Not because I'm worried about what he will say, but because I don't want him to deny me for the sake of my healing.

"Better than yesterday," I say, which isn't too far from the truth after covering myself in that miracle cream Justine gave me. Between the lidocaine in that stuff and the anti-inflammatories from the doc, my recovery is going far better than I imagined, but not quite as fast as I hoped.

Well, so long as I'm careful with my rib.

Luca closes the distance between us, and there's a rumble in his chest as he says, "Good. I've been dying to bend you over my desk for weeks."

His fingers are already undoing the button on my jeans, and I eagerly kick off my shoes, all thoughts of bodily pain completely forgotten. When he starts to jerk my pants down, I take over for him so he can undress himself, but he doesn't bother taking off his slacks.

By the time I'm naked from the waist down, his pants

are at his thighs and his hard cock is out. I reach to stroke him, but he turns me around, bends me over the desk, and smacks my ass hard enough that I'm certain there'll be an imprint there later. I take in a gasp and struggle to breathe.

Every part of my body aches from the action, but when he rubs his palm over the sore spot, all I can focus on is his touch and the way my pussy clenches in anticipation of him filling me.

In my next breath, his fingers rub over my clit, ensuring I'm ready, and before I can even gasp from the pleasure of his touch, his dick is thrusting inside me. He pushes down on my back with one hand, pressing me further onto his desk until I'm covering the papers left out.

My palms go flat over the hard surface as my legs spread wider, welcoming Luca's hand as he reaches around the front of me, his fingers putting pressure on my clit as he pounds into me.

"I want the whole house to hear you scream and know that you're mine, Raven." His murmured words have me trembling, barely able to keep standing and ready to explode from the inside out.

I take every thrust he gives with fervor and cry out his name as my orgasm draws closer. It's not going to take long today, and I'm sure the rest of my body will be thankful for that later.

The echoing slap from his hard thrusts fills the room alongside my moans, and I have to rest my head against the desk before I collapse in his arms. Even in my weakened state, he doesn't relent.

Luca owns every inch of me, taking control of my body without any resistance from me. The warmth pooling within my core grows bigger, spreading through my body with an urgency I can't control.

My nails scratch over the desk, looking for something to dig into and failing, but that doesn't take away from the pleasure coursing through me.

The moans turn to screams, and when Luca smacks my other ass cheek, I can't hold back any longer. Spots filter into my vision. I lose myself to the passion and trust that Luca has me when my legs feel as though they're becoming putty.

My breathing is ragged as I lay my cheek against the wood surface beneath me, and the jerky movements of Luca behind me confirm that he wasn't too far behind me. As he stills, his hands rub over my back, then down my ass, massaging my sore muscles.

It takes several minutes before the lightheadedness eases and I feel as though I can stand without fear of crumpling to the floor.

Luca pulls out of me and helps me rise. As soon as I stand, a sticky wetness drips between my thighs. I reach for a tissue from his desk before turning around. When I can see his face, there's a cocky grin there that has my own smile reappearing.

"Was that everything you hoped it would be?" I tease as he takes the tissues from my fingers.

One of his hands tightens around my hip, and the other slips between my legs to clean me up. "And then some."

I lean back, watching with admiration as he cares for me without missing a beat. Only when he's finished does he move to pull up his pants. "I have some more work to take care of, but I'll be done before dinner."

"Work for Monroe Investments or..." He hasn't said anything about Tori, but I can't leave his office without an update. Even if it's that nothing has changed.

"Monroe, but I checked in on Tori this morning," he replies, handing me my pants and underwear. "She's still doing fine from what we can tell. I just need a few more days, unless something points to her being in more danger."

As much as I want Tori out of that house, I trust Luca. So, instead of arguing with him, I nod with understanding. "I appreciate you keeping eyes on her."

"We have someone watching the house at all times," he says. "But what we're really hoping for is to get in touch with Bryson. I need to know what Titan's end game is and to make sure there aren't any contingencies set in place for when he fails. Once we have the information, that man will regret the day he chose to go after me and hurt you."

When he says those words, telling me that he's going to kill my father, I feel nothing but utter joy and peace that he'll soon no longer be walking this Earth... I know I'm right where I'm supposed to be.

19

OLIVIA

Three more days pass, and while I'm starting to go insane that Tori is still in the clutches of Titan, I'm at least healing and ready to make sure that I'm not left behind when it's time to go get my best friend.

Luca has been to meeting after meeting and working all hours of the day, but he seems certain that they'll be able to speak with Bryson soon. Certain plans have been put into motion, causing some chaos.

I lean my head back on my new tub and sigh contentedly. "Chaos, my ass. He means death."

I've learned quickly that Luca doesn't do anything without making a statement, and that usually ends with people dying. Bad people, but still. As I soak in the bubble bath for the first time since the bathroom remodel was finished in record time, I try to block out all other thoughts and just enjoy the fact that I was able to walk and bend over without wincing. More importantly, most of my bruises have faded to a barely visible yellow.

My eyes close and I wiggle my toes out of the water as my legs float upward. The bathroom is steamy from the hot water, and music plays from my phone on the counter. This could only be more perfect if I wasn't alone.

Then, as if my thoughts conjured the devil himself, I feel vibrations from the slamming of the front door moving through the apartment and hear Luca's heavy steps coming closer.

Still, I don't move or even open my eyes. This is my time, and unless he says we're moving on Tori, I don't intend to ask him for an update. I've learned that no news right now is the good kind, which I'm slowly becoming okay with.

I listen as he enters the bedroom, and I'm pretty sure I hear him go into the closet. There's some rustling around before his steps come closer to me.

My chest starts to tighten, and when he says my name gruffly, I'm pretty sure I stop breathing.

By the time I open my eyes, he's kneeling next to the bathtub with an intense look on his handsome face, and he's reaching for the back of my head. His fingers tangle in my already messy bun, jerking my upper body forward until our mouths collide.

Bubbles from the bath float around me as I move to get closer, tempted to drag his fully clothed ass into the water with me. As his tongue parts my lips, I reach up and grip his shirt, tugging him nearer and moaning into his mouth.

I'm becoming a sex addict, thanks to this man, but I can't get enough of him. Not now and likely not ever.

He deepens the kiss, angling my face and holding tighter to my hair, but just when I think he's about to take things further, he pulls back. "Fuck, Raven."

With the rough tenor of those two words, I know something is wrong and every bit of my rising libido is dashed away. "What's wrong?"

"It's time to move," he announces, rising from his kneeling position and grabbing my towel.

"Move?" I question, my heart rate increasing for all new reasons. "Like 'go get Tori' move?"

Luca holds the white, fluffy cotton material out for me. "Hopefully. We'll be setting the plan into motion. If the opportunity presents itself, we'll grab Tori at the same time."

"Is she okay?" I ask with panic in my voice as I stand from the water, stepping into the waiting towel. "What's the rush?"

Not that I don't want her back, but something feels wrong about this. Not only his hurry, but the tone of his voice and the crease between his eyes that seems to deepen with my hesitation.

"Everything is fine," he insists. "We've been waiting for a window, and now we have it. Be ready in three minutes or I'll need to leave without you."

Before he's even finished speaking, I move my ass into

gear, thankful that I didn't wash my hair yet. All I need to do is dry off and get new clothes on. I do the former on my way to the closet and grab underwear first, then a pair of black pants, then my socks and boots, followed by a light grey tank top since it's warmer outside and I don't feel the need to hide my fading bruises any longer.

With one minute to spare, I step out of the closet and head toward the living room to find Luca already at the front door, open and waiting. "Let's go."

My heart rate starts to pick up, and my palms go sweaty. I can't actually believe he's letting me come with him. Whatever this "chaos plan" is, I assume it's not dangerous. Or maybe he's now firm in the thought that separating us during shitstorms like this is worse than bringing me along.

Either way, I'm anxious to get Tori back safe and sound, but I don't like not knowing what's going to happen between now and then.

"What's the plan?" I ask once we're in the elevator, headed down toward the garage.

Luca's typing speedily on his phone, but still manages to answer me without missing a beat. "We're going to make a bomb go off."

My head whips back toward him so hard that my neck pops. "A what now?"

"An explosion, Raven," he drones. "A bomb that goes boom and freaks everyone the fuck out."

"Why in the hell would you do that?" I ask, panic clawing its way up my throat as my deranged mind conjures an image of Tori's mangled body having to be uncovered from beneath rubble. Yeah, super fucking helpful.

He doesn't answer me right away. Instead, his focus is back on his phone and I lose my patience when the elevator doors open to the garage. Before he can step out, I grip the front of his black shirt and force him to look at me.

"Why, Luca?" I demand.

His gaze moves toward where I'm grabbing him, something else he's probably not used to people attempting with him, but I can't give a single damn right now.

"It will be small and controlled," he answers. "Just enough to hurt Bryson, putting him in the hospital where we'll be able to get to him. If Titan let him go once, he should again."

I blink several times, trying to process the fact that Luca seems to think he can *control* every little thing and is about to put lives at risk.

"You can't do this," I say, but he begins walking forward, uncaring that I still have a hold on him. My hold breaks as soon as he gets two steps away.

"I can and I will," he replies. "If you don't want to be part of this, then I suggest you go back upstairs." He pauses and turns back to me when we're halfway to the waiting SUV. "I'd rather have you with me, but if you can't handle this, then stay and keep the door locked."

Dark eyes plead with me, a look I feel confident is

one he doesn't show very many people. Hell, possibly nobody else.

Luca asked before if I trusted him. When I said I did, I meant it. Reminding myself of that, I take a deep breath, force my nerves down, and shake my head. "I'm coming with you."

"Good." He grabs my hand and leads me forward, opening the door to the back seat of the waiting vehicle. "Now, get in. I'll be right back."

A little begrudgingly, I do so, but when the door slams closed behind me, I flip him off just to make myself feel better.

I'm sure Luca has done this before. Explosions or whatever. He did say "small and controlled." Maybe it will be more like firecrackers or something. My hands cover my face as I groan. "Fat fucking chance of that."

Luca returns at the same time that Markus slides into the driver's seat and Jaxon into the front passenger. I glance behind us, but nobody is moving to get in the rear. "It's just the four of us?"

That doesn't make me feel any better.

Luca shakes his head. "Damon is driving another SUV with a few others that will follow behind us, and there are two other crews waiting just a block away in case anything goes wrong."

"How many people work for you?" I realize then that I've seen or heard at least a dozen voices in this house, and only Luca, Jaxon, Justine, Damon, and Markus... well, and me, live at the compound.

He looks up at Jaxon, who's been unusually quiet, but answers my question. "Currently, there are forty-three people we would trust to call on if all hell broke loose, but we have over one hundred that say they're loyal to the Monroe family."

Another thing I find interesting. The Monroe family isn't made up of blood relatives like I would have thought when considering a mafia. Luca has made it seem as though he's the last living member of his family. No parents or grandparents or anything of the sort. Not that we've talked specifically about it.

Maybe that's something we need to chat about soon.

Jaxon's holding a purse in his lap, and because I can't help myself, I ask, "Why do you have that bag?"

He winks back at me. "It's to hide the bomb in."

I want to reply, but my voice is stuck in my throat along with all the air in my lungs. The bomb is in the fucking car. With us.

Mother fuck fuck.

Instead of sharing my displeasure at that, I stare out the window and watch where we're driving. I know even if I say something, nobody else sitting in the SUV will share my concern. Nor would any of them do anything about it.

I let the scenery of East Portland distract me. There are patches of trees in this neighborhood, and I sigh, not remembering the last time I got out of the city and enjoyed the quiet of nature. I'll need to rectify that just as soon as possible.

Tori and I used to enjoy drives to the coast and checking out the tidepools, taking bets on how many starfish we could find. The loser always had to drive home, and after being under the sun all day, driving was a bitch of a task.

Plans are already getting made in my head, distracting me from reality. I'll have Tori back, there will be no more secrets between us, and we'll enjoy a girls' day like we used to. Except this time, Justine will have to come. I have a feeling the two of them will enjoy driving me crazy and get along just fine.

Once Tori's initial rage has faded, that is. She's the more innocent, polite one out of the two of us, but I've seen when she's truly upset. It's something I've been equally fascinated by and terrified of throughout our decades-long friendship.

Markus pulls into a driveway, and the garage door opens. I glance around, even more confused. "Where are we?"

"A house that's only three away from Titan's and on the opposite side of the street," Luca answers, waiting for the garage door to lower before opening his door.

"And the people who live here just happened to not give a shit about letting you park here?" I ask, seeing the garage is filled with random totes and a few empty shelves.

"Technically, nobody lives here now." He reaches out a hand to help me out of the back seat. "I bought the house two days ago and everything they couldn't move out within twenty-four hours."

Once again, I'm not sure what to say to him. Just when I think I'm settling into this mafia life, unconcerned with murder, he continues to shock the hell out of me.

"You just...bought it and kicked them out?" I ask, not hiding my surprise.

He shrugs, leading me toward the interior door that Markus and Jaxon have already gone through. "I paid them nearly twice the value of the home. They'll be fine. And when this is all over, I'll turn it into a rental and eventually make my money back. For now, it serves the purpose of letting us hide out off the street."

The words all make sense. Shit, they even have logic, and while Luca basically said he was a billionaire the other day, my mind clearly hasn't wrapped itself around the fact that he just throws money around without blinking.

Sure, the compound, as the others call it, is nice, but there's nothing overly fancy about it. In fact, from the outside, it looks almost a little run down and more like a business building with underground parking than it does a home. I guess Luca has certain places he likes to spend his money, and his home isn't one of them.

When we enter the house, there's a short hallway that dumps out into a kitchen with light oak cabinets, all of them open and mostly empty. The fridge and even the stove are gone, and I can't see a single place to sit as I peek around for a dining table.

"I guess they know how to clear a place out," I muse.

"We won't be here long," Luca says, moving to stand next to Jaxon who not only has a small explosive device sitting on the counter in a brown and tan purse, but also has blueprints laid out over the granite counters.

Markus points to a spot on the page, but I can't tell what it is from where I'm standing. "We need to come in around this fence and place the bomb under this window. It should be contained to a twenty-foot radius, avoiding the neighboring houses and damaging everything on the left side of Titan's."

I push up onto my toes, trying to read the blueprint, but having no clue what I'm looking at. "Where is Tori going to be while all of this is going down?"

"Right here in the living room," Luca says, showing me, but on that paper, without a size reference, I have no clue if it's far enough away. "We have someone watching her now. She has the same routine nearly every day. About this time, she's always watching something on the television."

I glance at my phone and see it's just after eleven in the morning, then start to laugh. "Oh, that woman."

Luca raises a brow. "Do I need to know something?"

"Not that relates to what you're doing," I answer with a chuckle. "I just get to make fun of her when this is over for what she's been up to."

My best friend has a secret obsession with soap operas. She told me a couple years ago that she finally stopped watching, but I remember the schedule. I was always annoyed when she didn't want to have lunch with me. She's absolutely enjoying her drama shows.

They continue to dissect their plan, confirming all the little details that I don't need to know about. I distract myself with a quick tour of the house. Random garbage is left here and there, but overall, it's bigger than I would have expected.

Next to the dining room is a large family area with dark hardwood floors and a stained rug in the middle. Beyond that is another hallway which leads to a couple of bedrooms and stairs that go up, but before I can see what's upstairs, Luca is calling my name.

I return to the kitchen to find Jaxon with the purse on his arm and the blueprints rolled up on the counter, but it's Luca's gaze that I keep my focus on.

"We're going in," he says. "This is going to happen fast, and I need you to remain calm. You're here for several reasons, but the most important one is that we need you to get Tori and run straight back here. Wait in the SUV, count down for three minutes, and if we're not back yet, drive. The keys are still in the ignition."

I swallow hard at that last bit. "So, there's a chance this is all going to go to shit?"

He reaches for me and cups my cheek. "There's always a chance, but that's why we're prepared, so even if things don't go as we hope, we know what to do."

His relaxed and confident attitude is keeping me somewhat calm. I want to ask more questions, but before

I can open my mouth, he's pulling on my hand and we're exiting out the front door.

He wasn't wrong earlier about this moving fast. We've barely been here for five minutes, and the group is already splitting up, Jaxon still with the bomb.

My eyes follow his movements as I trust Luca to guide me to wherever I'm supposed to be. I'm suddenly jerked to the right and forced behind a mailbox that likely does a shitty job of hiding either of us.

"Someone is coming out the front door," Luca mutters, leaning around me. "Stay here and wait for my whistle."

He's gone in the blink of an eye, moving along the manicured shrubs. I try to watch, but he disappears from my view. Just as I'm certain my heart is about to escape from my chest, a body is thrown over a small fence into a yard just one house over from where we're headed.

Luca does his whistle, and I find myself working on autopilot since I'm too damn afraid at this point not to listen to every single thing he tells me to do. I run in the direction I saw him go, slowing only once I'm near the unconscious man.

I didn't think I remembered anyone who hurt me when Titan had possession of me, but the moment I lay eyes on this one, dark memories filter through my thoughts.

This...monster. He enjoyed throwing me into the wall, laughing and screaming simultaneously in my face and flickering the lights until I threw up. He was sadistic and cruel and—I want to kill him.

I don't even know how I can, but seeing him and no longer being the captive, I step closer without thinking. I'm nearly standing over his body when Luca finds me.

"What are you doing, Raven?" he asks, urgency in his voice that's overshadowed by curiosity.

My eyes stay on the still-unconscious man. "He hurt me."

My foot lifts without much thought. If I press my shoe over his throat, how long would I have to stand here before he suffocated?

I don't know the answer, but I want to.

Except Luca is pulling me away and I lose my footing, falling onto the grassy lawn. I open my mouth to voice my displeasure, but Luca is bent over the body and when his arm moves, his hand is holding a bloody knife.

He wipes it over his pants, then tucks the blade away before turning back to me. "We need to move."

My eyes don't leave the body until I have confirmation. I need to know that whoever he is, he can't hurt me or anyone else ever again.

When I see the crimson pooling around his chest from a gaping stab wound, I feel lighter than I expected. A peace fills me at knowing the world is a little safer without this stranger in it, and I willingly follow Luca to where he's taking me.

Funny how bombs freak me the fuck out, but dead bodies not so much.

We get to the next fence, and he stops, pointing at the next house. "That's where Tori is. She's still in the living room and out of the radius for the bomb. It's going off in two minutes, and it's going to be louder than you realize. Push past the shock you'll feel, go through the front door no sooner than twenty seconds after the explosion, grab Tori, and run. Don't explain anything to her until you're in the SUV. Do you understand?"

"Loud noises. Twenty seconds. Grab and run," I repeat the instructions, trying to hide my shaking hands from him. "I can do that."

"I know you can," he replies earnestly, "or you wouldn't be here. But I meant what I said earlier. Leave without us if we're not back within three minutes of you getting to the car. Not a second later."

"Got it." I tap my phone in my back pocket. "I'll even set a timer."

He glances behind us, then back at me. "Promise me, Raven. Three minutes."

"I promise." As the words leave my mouth, my chest constricts to the point of causing me physical pain, but I don't get the chance to dwell for long.

Luca's lips press to mine, his tongue tasting me for the briefest of seconds, then he's pulling away and turning to walk in the opposite direction.

I watch his retreating form, trying to get my anxiety under control, something that doesn't happen until he looks back one last time and nods at me. His final confirmation that he trusts me and has faith I can complete the task I've been given.

That isn't a cure-all for my nerves, but it's the boost I need as I crouch lower to the ground and wait for the bomb to go off.

20

LUCA

W alking away from Olivia, leaving her to do what only she can accomplish quietly, without resulting in injury for Tori, is the last thing I wanted to do, but when we came up with this plan yesterday, I knew we couldn't do it without her.

Two things need to happen right now: Bryson needs to be injured enough to go to the hospital again, and Tori needs to escape. While I can handle Bryson, none of us were going to be able to get Tori out without hurting her in the process. None of us except Olivia.

Jaxon is setting the bomb, and I'll be right behind him. Bryson made this personal when he wrote that note and I need to be certain that this plan goes as it should. Markus is watching the front of the house with two others. His most important job will be making sure Olivia doesn't run into any issues.

While the job I've given her has to be done on her own, she won't be alone.

Damon and his crew are on the backside of the house, watching for Titan to escape. If he does, we'll grab him, but no one is going in the house further than the hole we put in the wall outside of what I presume is Bryson's room, thanks to the recon my men have been doing over the last five days.

So far, outside of killing that man for Olivia, everything has gone to plan. Though, I can't help wondering if I hadn't gone back for her, what would she have done?

Stabbing his heart was nothing for me, and I expected a bit more of a reaction from her, but even when she told me he was one of the men who hurt her, there was very little emotion in her voice or on her face.

It's something I think the two of us need to talk about. Not that I could possibly shame her for wanting him dead, but if she's going to have a thirst for the blood of her enemies, then I need to know. Mostly so I can help and she doesn't end up putting herself into a situation that she can't get out of.

My phone vibrates with a text.

Jaxon: Bag in place. Be where you're supposed to be and nobody will lose a limb.

Considering it seems as if Titan has welcomed an attack on this house, I don't hide behind anything. I stand on the opposite side of the yard from where I know

Olivia is hunched down and stay within the shadows. If someone walked out the front door, they'd see me, but for the moment, I'm safe here.

It has frustrated me to no end that I haven't figured out Titan's endgame and why he's all of a sudden not running from me. After today, hopefully all of that will change.

Bryson is the key. He has to be. Otherwise, I don't understand the point of the note he left for me with that nurse.

I watch the clock and then the house where I can see the bag peeking out from behind a grouping of flowers that I don't know the name of. Though, I'm certain my Raven does.

There's a beep, and the ground beneath my feet shakes with the force of the explosion. Brick siding from the house scatters across the yard with glass mixed in. Smoke billows up from the hole in the wall, and shouts start within the house.

As much as I want to watch for Olivia and make sure she gets where she's supposed to be, I need to trust Markus to do his job while I do mine.

After just a few seconds, I run toward the newly made hole, noticing Jaxon coming from around the side of the house to watch my back. We have to be quick. I have no doubts Titan and his men will be here within moments. I'm only going to make sure the bomb did its job and provide a distraction for Olivia to get Tori.

I walk over the rubble, glancing left and right. I don't see anyone in the room, so I move in further. The lights are off, but it's midday and I can see well enough. When I look around the bed, the floor there is empty.

"Fuck," I hiss. I'm going to have to go further into the house and do the job myself, which complicates things and puts me at risk of not getting back to Olivia in time, but we have a backup plan for that, too.

I push forward and hear Jaxon behind me. "Plan B?"

"Yep."

"I got your back," he assures me, but it's not necessary. I already know he would die for me. Otherwise, he wouldn't be here.

As soon as I step into the hallway, a force collides with me. Both of us teeter from the impact, but I grab onto the shirt of the man in front of me, drawing my gun. I'm a half-second from putting a bullet through his skull when my eyes meet his.

Bryson.

He's right here. After all these years. The more rage-filled part of me still wants to shoot him, but the logical part of my brain wins out. I press the gun to his side instead of his head.

"What are you doing here?" he seethes, glancing back at his room.

"Doing a bit of remodeling," I answer, then add quietly, "I'll see you at the hospital later."

His head tilts to the side, then I shoot him.

Not what I planned, but it works for the situation. He

won't die. As long as he gets a doctor to pull the bullet from his ribs. A little payback for beating on Olivia and for abandoning me all those years ago without a word.

Men come into the hallway from all sides, including Titan. Jaxon starts shooting, and I throw Bryson to the ground, half in his room so he'll likely avoid any stray shots.

My eyes lock with Titan's. He's just standing there, not making a move to retaliate against our actions as he grins at me. His smirk pisses me the fuck off, because I don't know what he does. But I will soon. That fucker isn't going to get away with whatever he's been planning. I'll make damn sure of that.

"We need to go," Jaxon tells me just a moment later.

I step back, kicking Bryson on my way out and moving quicker through the rubble. My eyes cast around the yard, but I don't see Olivia or Markus.

Fuck. I hope they made it out.

The house is wide enough that by having eyes on Titan just now, he should at least not have seen Olivia sneak in, but I don't know if he would have sent someone else to get Tori and lock her up somewhere.

When we pass the front door, it's wide open and so are the curtains in the living room. I don't see anyone, and there aren't any messages on my phone that something has gone wrong. Still, as I continue past the house, further away from Titan, allowing him to live, I can't help from thinking.

Even if everything went how we hoped, or close

enough, did we just do exactly what he was hoping we would? And if we did, how the fuck could he use that to his advantage?

21

OLIVIA

As soon as the explosion goes off, I take a steady breath and start the timer on my phone. My eyes shift between the countdown, Luca, and the massive fucking hole in the side of the once-beautiful house. Someone—likely Tori—screams, Luca and Jaxon are entering the house, and then it's my time to move.

I stand from my position at the fence and run for the front door while giving my surroundings a onceover. I don't see anyone through the living room, not even Tori, but that doesn't stop me from going to the front door and pushing it open.

A few seconds pass and nobody comes running to see who threw the door open, making me feel confident to move forward. I go right to the living room and there's a step down to where the couch sits, angled toward the massive television on the wall.

The power must have been blown when the bomb

went off since everything in here is dark, but I can see well enough, thanks to the oversized windows. Still, I don't spot Tori.

I know I have mere seconds to grab her and run. Thanks to that short time, I start to panic, having no clue where to look for her. But I refuse to give up. Not when I'm so close to having her back and the peace of mind that she won't be hurt at some point by Titan.

Moving around the couch, I notice a small hallway that leads to another room. When I step across the threshold, a fist slams into my stomach, thankfully avoiding my busted rib, followed by a screech.

"Damn it, Tori," I groan. "It's me."

Before she can hit me a second time, she pauses with her fist in the air. "Olivia?" Her eyes widen, tears filling them. "Olivia!"

She moves to hug me, but I recover from her punch and grab her wrist. "We need to hug it out later. Come on."

Her feet remain planted. "We can't leave. Your dad... He's..."

"I know, Tor." My eyes plead with her to not make this harder than it needs to be. "But if you trust me at all, if our friendship means anything to you, don't ask questions. Just run with me. Please."

She glances around, hands shaking and lip quivering. "We need to find your dad."

"My dad died the day he walked out on me, then again when he beat the shit out of me for not doing what he wanted me to only last week," I say curtly. "Now, come with me."

I turn to make sure we're still alone and see Markus enter the house. His eyes land on me and then Tori. She whimpers behind me, and I know if I don't get her to come willingly, Markus has likely been sent to make sure she's brought with us by any means necessary.

My fingers squeeze Tori's tightly, and I practically growl at her. "Tori, we're out of time."

Without waiting for her response, I keep my grip secure on her hand and yank. She follows after me, and just when we get to the front door, I hear a gunshot, which makes my steps quicken, and thankfully Tori's, too.

"What the hell is happening?" she asks, voice rough. I have no doubt she's crying as we run, but there's no time to placate her. Luca gave me instructions, and I'll be damned if I don't follow them.

"Five minutes," I say without glancing over at her. "Give me five minutes and I will answer every question truthfully. I promise."

She continues to run, now next to me with her longer stride, and doesn't say anything else. When we get to the house where the SUV is waiting for us, I storm through the front door and into the garage. Before I open the door, I pull my phone out again and set another timer. This one is for three minutes, and I have a feeling they're going to be the longest of my life.

"Get in the back," I tell Tori, and she surprisingly

does as I say. Glancing behind me, I expect to see Markus, considering he was right there when we exited the house, but he's nowhere to be seen.

The seconds tick down, and before the first minute is up, Tori pops her head out of the back door. "Care to tell me what the hell we're doing and why we aren't driving away?"

"I'm waiting for Luca. If he's not back in," I look at the screen, "two minutes, three seconds, I'll drive us away from here."

Tears still fill her eyes, but at the mention of his name, tension lines her face. "Luca, as in the man that kidnapped you and has been using your life against your dad's for years?"

"What in the actual fuck has he been telling you?" I mean, technically, Luca did kidnap me, but having used me against Titan? That I wouldn't believe even if the Pope told me himself.

"Christopher told me everything, Liv," she says, using the name I thought for years was my father's given one, but who the hell knows now. Titan, Christopher, doesn't make a fuck of a difference to me. He still needs to die for what he's done.

My stare is hard when I meet Tori's again, and I'm not the least bit concerned about being considerate with my words, even though she doesn't know the truth yet. "Christopher is a piece of shit father who is going to die, and I hope I'm there to see it happen."

She gasps and flinches back from me. "What happened to you?"

I know I've gone too far. Tori's too damn sensitive for all of this. I knew that weeks ago, and that's why I never told her what I'd gotten caught up in. My anger made me think I momentarily didn't care, but when she refuses to look at me again, the guilt weighs heavy on me.

There's less than a minute left now, and I jump into the front seat. Without looking back at her, I say, "Close your door and buckle up."

She doesn't verbally acknowledge my request, but the door at least closes, and I press the button on the garage opener clipped to the visor. When the doors start to roll up, I put the SUV in reverse, and everything inside me protests at the thought of leaving Luca behind.

The more sensible part of me has no doubt that he's set up contingency plans, but the more emotional part, the pieces of me that fell for Luca the moment he even looked at me, fights against the thought of driving away.

Still, logic wins out and I reverse down the driveway, turning the wheel to head in the direction opposite Titan's house. My stomach churns and my hands shake as I move to put the SUV into drive. Once I do, I hear sirens coming closer and know we're out of time.

One glance in the rearview mirror and my heart sinks when I don't see Luca or anyone else running toward us.

"Fuck," I mutter, lifting my foot off the brake and toward the gas pedal.

Before I can press down, a hand smacks on the

window and I scream as if I've been shot. I nearly slam on the gas anyway, but when I look up, I'm glad my instincts didn't have me racing away.

Luca stands there, chest heaving. "Move."

He opens the door, and I slide the seat back to pull my legs up and climb over the center console, into the passenger's seat.

The back door opens during all that, and Jaxon joins Tori in the back. He says something that I miss, but then chuckles. "Too soon. Got it. Just so you know, it almost always is with me."

Tori's arms are crossed and she's staring out the window, pressed against the door. She looks more pissed than scared, which I hope is a good thing. Though, the longer I stare at her, the more I remember my first time in this SUV. I sat in almost the same position, probably just as scared, if not more.

My arm reaches into the back seat as Luca drives away, and I touch Tori's knee with the tips of my fingers, but she jerks further away. Her glare cuts toward me. "Not now, Olivia."

Oh, hell. I've crossed a line. I knew this was going to happen, but still, I hoped we could have a little reunion before she screamed at me.

Since Tori doesn't want to yell at me yet, I give my attention to Luca. "Did everything go as you planned?"

His jaw is tight, and I only see a small amount of blood splatter glinting off his black shirt from the sun.

"Sure." His tone is clipped, and the addition of a tic in his cheek tells me not to ask any other questions.

Great. He's pissed off, too. This is just how I saw my day going when I started it with a soak in the new bathtub.

I lean back in my seat and close my eyes. Just as I'm trying to clear my mind, a hand settles on my shoulder.

"Don't worry," Jaxon says cheerily. "Nobody died, and even if your friend hates you right now, at least she's safe. She'll thank you later."

Tori scoffs but continues to give me the silent treatment.

I'm tempted to correct Jaxon and tell him someone did in fact die. It just didn't happen inside the house. Though, something tells me that casually chatting about murder right now isn't going to help my situation with Tori.

Jaxon leans back in his seat, and I go back to calming my racing heart. The danger should be mostly behind us. Still, something went wrong or happened that pissed off Luca. I knew we weren't going to be done with Titan, but I have a feeling things may have only gotten worse, even if everything went as planned. Or close to.

When we're back at the compound, Luca puts the SUV in park and reaches for my hand for the first time since we began driving. "I'll head to my office. You and Tori can go to the apartment."

Time to get yelled at. Great.

Jaxon is already out of the car, and when Luca exits,

Tori still won't look at me, so I get out, too, and head around to the other side to open her door. When I go to pull the handle, she hits the lock button.

"Oh, for fuck's sake." I sigh. "We're not ten."

I can't see her face, thanks to the tinted windows, but I know she's there and staring back. I don't budge and I don't dare walk away.

"Aren't you ready to scream at me and tell me all the reasons I should have stayed with daddy dearest back there?" I taunt, even though it pains me a little to do so.

The last thing I want to do is hurt Tori, but I already know things need to get worse between the two of us before they get better. That might be for an hour or a week or even a month. However long it takes, those are consequences I'm going to take in stride, because at the end of the day, Tori is my best friend. I'm not giving up on her just because she's rightfully angry with me.

Putting the final nail in my coffin, I roll my eyes and throw my hands in the air dramatically. "You know what? Screw you, Tori. You have no idea what I've been through, and for you to ignore me is an utter betrayal to our friendship. If you—"

She shoves the door open so hard that it nearly smacks into my face before I jump back. The fury in her eyes, the rapid rise and fall of her chest, and the red in her face tells me that my plan worked a little too well.

"Screw me?" she bellows. "Screw *me?* No, *fuck you.* You show up after abandoning me, either by choice or whatever is going on here, and then think we can just pick back up where we left off when you kidnap me? Not a chance in hell."

She slams the door closed and stomps toward the elevator, muttering and huffing as she goes. When her finger stabs at the call button, she says, "You better be following me or so help me God, I will..."

Her sentence trails off, because she's too kind to have a proper threat come to her. Naturally, I fight a smile as I walk toward her and step in behind her once the doors open.

I reach to press the fourth-floor button, and she stands as far away from me as she can. "Just because I'm coming in doesn't mean I'm staying."

"You're welcome to leave whenever you'd like," I say. "But only after you've heard me out."

When she huffs out dramatically, I have to hide my grin. This is going to be...fun.

22

OLIVIA

We get into the apartment, and instead of going to the couch to sit, Tori heads for the table across the room. I opt for a stop at the bar first and make two drinks. I have a feeling we're going to need them.

A bit of vodka, some cranberry juice along with pomegranate juice, then I stir both drinks before bringing them to the table.

When I set Tori's in front of her, she pushes it away. "You're not going to get me drunk in hopes that I'll forgive you easier."

"That wasn't my intent, but now that you say something," I joke, because that's what we do. Or at least used to. I'm the only one smiling.

I sit down and take a long pull from my drink. She may not need something to take the edge off, but after nearly killing someone, watching an explosion, kidnapping my best friend, and having to make the choice to leave Luca behind... I allow myself a moment to enjoy the sugary cocktail before beginning this inevitable fight.

With my hands clasped in front of me, I stare at Tori, even though she's still refusing to look at me. "Let's start at the beginning. I went to that auction, grieving and nervous beyond all reason, but I won. I got the highest bid of the night. When it was time to get the hell out of there, I was over being around people, so I headed toward the back of the hotel."

I watch Tori's face. While she's still not meeting my gaze, I at least feel confident that I have her full attention as she fiddles with her fingers over the table.

"When I went out a back exit, I was distracted with my phone. By the time I looked up, the door behind me was closed with no way back in, there was a dead body on the ground that just happened to be our senator, and people started to shoot at me."

Her head snaps up finally. "So, your dad was right. Luca tried to kill you."

"No," I say firmly. "In fact, Luca saved my life that night, but I won't sugarcoat things. He did take me against my will. I was brought back here, locked in a cell, and left by myself for a day or two."

"And still, you defend him?" She laughs, but the sound isn't filled with joy. "What happened to you, Liv?"

"My mother died, I saw a dead body, and I was kidnapped. Twice. And let me tell you, the second go-around courtesy of Titan made what Luca did seem like heaven," I reply tersely. "All of that changed me, but I need you to hear me out."

She presses her lips together and this time doesn't turn away as I continue.

"Even though I was a prisoner, essentially, Luca provided me with everything I asked for, and there's another woman here. Her name's Justine. She helped a lot, too. She's actually who you were texting with when I was still...not allowed to have my phone."

Tori's hand smacks the tabletop. "I knew something was off with you. I chalked it up to the grief, but I should have pressed harder."

I can see the guilt in her eyes, but it's not necessary.

"This isn't your fault," I say. "It just happened, and I don't regret it. Luca took care of me. He paid all the bills at my mother's house and made sure my apartment was emptied out before I lost anything. All without me asking or even telling me, because he didn't want me to feel obligated to stay with him."

"He's a psychopath, Liv," she sneers. "Whatever he did, it was only to get in your head and make you think that he's the good guy."

My anger is rising, but I remind myself that Titan has been fucking with her mind for days. He's someone she thought she could trust. Luca is a stranger to Tori, but I'll be damned if I don't change her mind.

I pull out my phone and show her pictures of my face and body from the day after I woke up. "Would a good guy do that?"

She snatches the phone and zooms in. "I'll fucking kill him."

"That's exactly what I want to do, too," I say, taking my phone back.

Her brows pinch together. "I don't understand."

"Titan did that to me. Or Christopher, as we used to know him as," I tell her. "He sent people into this building, shot the place up, and then convinced one of Luca's men to get me out of this apartment where I was safe and take me to him. Once Titan had me, he killed Luca's man and kidnapped me. I was with him for several days, beaten, starved, and nearly killed until I escaped."

She rubs her temples and shakes her head. "This doesn't make any sense. Are you sure? You weren't drugged and confused?"

"No," I snap, standing from the table before I reach across and attempt to choke some sense into her. "I know what happened to me, Tori. And when I found out that Titan had you, I raged on your behalf, and Luca spent days figuring out the best way to free you with the least amount of risk. He is the good guy here. Maybe not a saint. I won't lie, he's the leader of a mafia family, but he's not evil. Not like Titan."

Tori stays at the table while I pace further away. My frustration is getting the better of me. I don't understand how she can't believe me. I don't know what I'm supposed to do to convince her that Luca isn't the one we need to be afraid of.

"Why didn't you tell me any of this before?" she

demands, turning in her seat to face where I stand in the living room. "Why would you lie to me and tell me that you were basically vacationing from your problems and enjoying the wealth of some man who won you at auction? You told me nothing and Chris—Titan, whatever, said all these things... What do you expect me to do?"

Her voice is nearing yelling. This is what I expected, and she's not wrong. I lied to her, and she has every right to be mad about that.

"I'm sorry that I lied," I say sincerely. "I was trying to protect you from all of this. You and murderers and guns... I didn't see that working out so well. I also knew that you would have tried to get me to leave when that isn't what I wanted or want now."

She shoots out of her seat and throws her arms into the air. "Of course I would have, Liv! Look around you. You're living with blood money. Even if Luca is 'good' as you say, he still hurts people. I know losing your mom hurt like hell. I grieved right alongside you. But this?" She gestures around the room. "This isn't a good coping mechanism."

"I'm not coping," I reply. "I'm *living*. For the first time in much too long, I feel alive. Like I'm where I'm meant to be. All of this doesn't scare me, and I understand that it's not for you, but don't try and take it away from me."

My hands shake at my sides, and I want to throw

something, but I focus on my breathing instead. I just need to let her be furious so she can calm the fuck down.

"So, you want me to just be okay with the fact that on any given day you could be killed?" She crosses her arms and stares me down, but I'm not afraid. Not anymore.

"Yes, that's exactly what I want," I say softer. "I want you to support me, and if you can do that, then I won't have to lie to you or hide the truth. We can still be best friends. You can be in my life, and I can be in yours, but I'm with Luca now. I need you to know that Titan is the fucked-up one. The one I hope to see die for what he did to me and likely would have done to you had his plan not worked."

Her eyes fill with tears, and she covers her face with both hands as she settles back into the dining chair. "Damn it, Liv."

Any flicker of frustration immediately leaves me, and I rush toward her, wrapping my arms around her shoulders as I kneel in front of her chair. "I'm sorry. I love you and I'm sorry. I'll say that as many times as you need to hear it. I don't want to lose you, but I also need you to accept me."

Her body shakes within my hold, and she doesn't reply, but I know she needs this. She sobs over my shoulder, and eventually, I join her. The tears fall and they don't stop, minute after minute.

We hold each other, letting out the pain, rage, and fear that I'm certain we've both been feeling for much too long now. All caused by the same things, but for different reasons.

When she finally pulls back, her eyes rimmed with red, I'm sure mine match. We wipe at our faces and finally smile at each other. She drags me back into another hug. "I've missed you so much."

"I missed you, too," I reply sincerely as I move to stand up, taking her with me.

She reaches back first. "I think I'll have that drink now."

We both laugh, and I can breathe again. I know things aren't going to go back to the way they were, but I'm certain the worst is out of the way. She can yell at me some more later. For now, I just need my best friend.

We take our drinks to the couch and sit down facing each other. Tori puts a hand on my knee and smiles. Though, I don't miss the bit of force behind the action.

"If you're so taken with this guy," she says, "I'm going to need you to tell me more good stuff. And if you leave anything out this time, there's a chance I may not forgive you."

I reach for her hand and squeeze her fingers. "I won't leave a single detail out, even when you tell me to."

She throws her head back and groans. "What have I signed up for?"

"A crazy fucking ride."

23

LUCA

I knew that Tori would have reservations about leaving Titan's house, but I didn't expect her to hold resentment toward Olivia. Several times on the drive back, I was tempted to reach back and give her a piece of my mind, but I knew Olivia wouldn't have appreciated that.

Instead, I've given them their space to sort their shit privately while I finalize plans for the remainder of the day. My stomach still churns with an unease that I'm not accustomed to. I was aware that Titan was waiting for us to attack and didn't put too much thought into why he'd finally left himself vulnerable by staying somewhere we knew the location of.

Now that we've been there and done what we needed to but didn't have him put up a fight, I know I'm missing something. They barely shot back, and not a single vehicle followed us. On top of that, I heard the cops coming, but our group was the only one that fled.

Why? I need to know what the fuck we just walked into before it blows up in my face.

In my office, I go to my side table where I keep a few bottles of bourbon and Scotch and pour myself a hefty drink while I wait for Jaxon, Damon, and Markus to meet me here.

My fingers drum over the full glass as I consider what we could have possibly missed, but fuck if I can think of anything. I don't know if it's because he's just too many damned steps ahead of me, which is infuriating beyond reason, or if he's just that fucking stupid.

I hope for the latter, but I need to be prepared for the former. If Titan has bested us, knowing how will be essential in getting back at him. Or more accurately, killing him without everything else around me imploding.

Markus returns first, and I get him a Scotch. He accepts it with a nod. "That went almost too well."

And the boulder in my gut only gets bigger.

"I know." We clink glasses and I down half my contents in one swallow. "What are we missing?"

He shrugs, and even though I don't expect an actual answer, I need ideas, possibilities, anything to have this make sense.

I hear the mumbles of Damon's and Jaxon's voices. Neither of them seems happy, which helps my mood.

Two more glasses are poured, and the four of us sit

around my desk. Me behind it and them sitting in front of me.

"What the fuck was that?" Damon demands. "I didn't get to shoot a single person."

I smirk and shake my head. "How pitiful. Any thoughts as to why that is?"

Jaxon raises his glass, and my eyes go to him. For as much of a pain in my ass he can be at times, the bastard is rather insightful.

"We're being set up," he says.

I raise my brow when he doesn't continue. "How so?"

"I thought that he was waiting for us to attack so he could blow us to shreds with something we wouldn't expect, but I don't think he's going for an actual kill here," Jaxon says. The weight I've been carrying instantly gets heavier.

"That motherfucker wants to ruin me," I say, finally having a piece of the missing information I couldn't conjure myself.

Jaxon nods. "I don't know how, but think about it. You stole his daughter. He then 'rescued' Tori and we stole her away while also blowing up his house. He's going to use that against you."

"But how?" I ask, still not seeing the full picture.

The cops would have been here by now if he'd stayed behind to tell them who attacked their house, but nothing of the sort has happened.

What the fuck is he waiting for?

"That's what we need Bryson for," Damon says, then finishes off the rest of his drink as he stands to pour another.

He's not wrong, and waiting until tonight to go see him is going to make for a long fucking day.

"So, that's it," I say. "We know Titan is planning something big and that we might have fallen right into his trap, but there's nothing we can do until tonight?"

"That's not entirely true," Markus replies. "Why do we need to wait until tonight and give Titan more time to act? He's outwardly trying to fuck us, so why do we need to hide? Let's go see Bryson now and get the information we need."

Bryson said he was trying to protect someone else within Titan's grasp and that he couldn't out himself yet. I had respected that before, but Markus is right. We don't have time to waste. Bryson better have sorted his shit out, because we're coming for him, and he's going to cooperate whether he wants to or not.

"Get ready," I say, then glance at Jaxon. "See if he ended up at the same hospital or somewhere else. With a bullet wound, there's no way he didn't go somewhere."

He's already out of his seat and has his phone in hand. "You got it. I'll be in the garage within ten minutes."

Damon and Markus both agree, and our plans are set. This shit is going to end and really fucking soon. I'm done with Titan's games. He needs to die today.

I leave my office with the rest of them and hope that Olivia has had enough time to calm Tori down, because I need to get into my room.

After going up the elevator, I head to my door, and when I hear laughter, I don't bother knocking. Entering the apartment, I find Olivia and Tori on the couch together, each of them with a drink in hand and tears in their eyes but smiles on their faces.

Olivia's bright stare meets mine, and she sobers. "Is everything okay?"

"We're heading to the hospital now," I say, moving toward my room.

She gets up to follow me as I assumed she would. My Raven doesn't just let things go. She seems to rather enjoy being pushy for information.

"Why so soon?" she asks once I enter the closet.

I start to undress from the black fatigues so I can change into my preferred suit. "Because we don't have time to wait. Titan is fucking with us, and I need answers now."

She watches me, standing just outside the door of the closet, and when I take a second to look at her, my dick starts to harden. "Unless you want your friend to hear you get fucked against the wall, I would quit looking at me like that."

Not that I have time to devour her, but I would make time.

Her cheeks fill with crimson. "As fabulous as that

sounds, you seem in a hurry." She leans against the doorframe. "What can I do?"

"You can stay here, question Tori about anything she may have overheard in that house, and relay it to me through text," I reply, buttoning up a white dress shirt.

Her eyes flick toward me briefly. "I've already done a bit of that. She said he was always kind. Never raised his voice and explained that the extra men were for their protection, hired help, not his regular crew."

She moves to face me again before continuing. "He even told her that you went as far as threatening my innocence and life after your father died, and that's why he had to leave. That he only did so to protect me and my mother."

As the words leave her mouth, I watch her eyes, all while the fury in my chest grows and expands through the rest of my body. My pants are still unbuttoned, but I stop everything I'm doing to stalk toward her.

My hands cup her face, and I hold her cheeks tight, keeping her gaze. "You know that's not true."

She nods. "Of course, I do. Though, I have a feeling it will take Tori some time to accept the truth."

"I don't give a fuck about your friend or what she thinks of me," I seethe. "All I need to know is that you know what's real, and it's not anything that piece of shit has spewed."

Olivia pushes up on her toes and presses her lips to mine. "I know, Luc. I'm here and I trust you and I'm not going anywhere."

Her actions and words only serve to increase my rage. While I believe her, it makes me want to kill Titan all that much more.

"Good." I kiss her once more, slipping my tongue between her lips and tasting her even though time isn't on our side. "I can't lose you, Raven. I'll destroy him for trying to take you from me."

"You have me," she murmurs. "All of me."

Fuck. I want to strip her naked and bend her over my bed so I can have my way with her. But until we have the whole story, the luxury of ravaging this stunning woman is going to have to wait.

"When I get home, I expect you to be naked and waiting for me in this bed," I say firmly, holding her shoulders until she nods. "You're mine tonight. Have Justine help you find Tori somewhere to sleep. I'm not sharing you."

She shudders within my hands and tugs her lip into her mouth, looking up at me with lustful eyes. "I think that can be managed."

I turn her around, smack her ass, then whisper in her ear, "It better be."

She totters out of the room, and I finish getting ready. I have a man to question and another to kill.

WE GET TO THE HOSPITAL, EACH OF US DRESSED LIKE the respectable businessmen we choose to portray on the outside, and head straight to room 1437, thankfully at a different hospital than before. I wasn't looking forward to seeing either of those nurses, but I would have dealt with them if I had to.

When we find Bryson's room, I'm mildly surprised to see that there isn't anyone waiting outside the door. I half figured that they still didn't trust him, but apparently, whatever Bryson has been worried about seems to be unfounded.

I motion for Damon, Jaxon, and Markus to wait outside the room, and I notice the latter two continue walking, likely doing their best to blend in. Three imposing men standing outside the room of a shooting victim probably isn't the best idea.

Entering the sterile room, I see Bryson with his eyes closed on a hospital bed. His face is slack, and there are a few days of facial hair around his cheeks. He's wearing a blue gown, and there's an IV in his arm that leads to a blood bag.

I kick his bed, and he groans. "What the..."

"Hello, Bryson," I say, the words quiet yet menacing.

He blinks several times and moves his stare between me and the door. "You can't be here."

"Yet here I am, and I'm not leaving until you tell me what I want to know," I reply, pulling a chair closer to his bedside.

Casually, I unbutton my suitcoat, take my seat, and bring my leg up to rest my ankle over my other knee while leaning back in the firm chair. "So, tell me. What happened today?"

He sneers at me. "You're being reckless. I expected better of you."

"I'm taking charge, Bryson," I correct. "You may have forgotten that since it's taken you over a decade to make contact, but this is what a real man looks like. Someone who doesn't sit by, waiting for things to happen to him. I make them happen for me. Now, you're going to tell me what I need to know, or I'm going to kill you like I should have the day you ran away with your head up your ass."

"You have no idea what you're talking about," he says, his eyes narrowing.

My hands pull apart, palms facing up as I say, "Then, enlighten me. Quickly."

He glances at the door once again, and I add, "Nobody is coming that shouldn't be. I've made sure of that."

"I told you not to underestimate Titan," he replies. "He has eyes in places you would never think."

"That doesn't make him someone I need to be afraid of," I say confidently.

Bryson smirks. "There's some of your dad in you after all. You may not be afraid of Titan, but he's been coming after you since the moment you took over for your father, taking from him what he thought to be rightfully his."

"What the fuck does that mean?" I demand. Considering I'd never even heard of Titan before a few years ago, I haven't the slightest clue how I could have taken anything from the man.

"Titan was born Christopher Danes," Bryson begins, speaking softly. "He grew up with your father, and Titan was his nickname from their school days. They were like brothers until he met Scarlett. He told your father that he needed a break from the life, and by the time that break was over, she was pregnant."

"With Olivia," I add, piecing things together in my own way as he speaks.

"Yes," he continues. "Titan reclaimed his life as Christopher, promising your father that he'd always be there for him when he needed him most. Over the years, Titan would show up for certain things, and then he'd disappear, but he got himself into trouble and your father refused to bail him out."

"And Titan didn't take that well." My chest expands as I take a deep breath. "Did he kill my father?"

Bryson shakes his head. "Not with his own hands, but he set things in motion. Told this person that and another this. Before any of us knew what was happening, your dad was in over his head, trying to fix the chaos, even though he had no clue how any of it had transpired.

"The day your father died, Titan showed up at the compound to take his place as the new Monroe leader, but he'd forgotten about you. He didn't realize how much respect you had with the men at such a young age. He had to change his plan—and quickly—before it all unraveled."

Olivia lost her father the same day I did. I never put the timelines together, but now that I'm hearing all this, I don't know how neither of us ever connected the two events.

He continues, "I was a little like Titan, and he knew it, except I was trying to have my cake and eat it too."

"What does that mean?" I ask, leaning forward and resting my elbows on my knees.

A wince escapes him as he tries to move as well. "I had a family. An incredible woman and a son."

My head cocks to the side. "How would I not know about that?"

"Only your father did," he answers. "I told him I wouldn't leave like Titan so long as he kept my secret. I split my time, careful to keep my two lives separate, but someone found out."

"Titan did." That fucking bastard. "He killed your family."

Bryson looks away and out the window behind me. "He killed my Gina and took my son. I don't know if he was only trying to punish me or replace the family he left behind, but he gave me a choice. I could either come with him willingly or forfeit my son's life."

"Why you?" I ask. "How could you help whatever he was trying to accomplish?"

His gaze meets mine again. "Time after time, Titan underestimated you. He's been trying to sabotage you since day one. His first attempt was taking me away, leaving you to rebuild an empire without a father figure.

"It took years," Bryson continues. "It wasn't until Monroe Investments became a Fortune 500 company that he realized he had to think smarter, playing the long game, and not just trying to take you down, but to ruin you."

"So, you've been there all this time, raising your son, and working for him to do what?" I demand. "Why haven't you stopped any of this?"

I'm two seconds from killing Bryson myself after hearing what he's had to say. All of this could have been stopped years ago if he'd just been a man and taken care of the fucking problem.

Then, he says, "Titan kept his word when I went with him. He didn't kill my son, but he has no clue I'm his father."

"What the fuck does that mean?"

"It means that Jerod believes Titan is his dad. One slip up from me, and Titan will kill him," Bryson says, a rumble to his words that matches my own ire. "My son has been dangled in front of me for years, being conditioned into a man he never should have been, and there's been nothing I could do about it."

"You could have come to me," I seethe, wanting to yell the words and punch him in the face for his stupidity.

"It was too late," he says, sounding more pathetic than the man I remember him to be. "I've done my best, Luc. I protected you as much as I could, but I've had to put my son first, even if he has no clue who I am. At least not in the way he should."

Fucking hell. This is twisted in more ways than I could have ever thought, but he still hasn't answered the most important question.

"What is Titan planning now?" I ask, trying to keep my rage in check before Bryson decides he should keep this information to himself.

He nods at the door. "Go close it. I'm sure it's too late now and Titan already knows you're here, but I'd rather be careful."

I do as he asks, noticing Damon's grim face as I do. He's been listening, but I don't mind. It will save me from having to repeat myself later.

When I return, I don't bother to sit. I'm ready to get the hell out of here as soon as he answers my last question.

"Titan baited you into attacking the house today," Bryson begins. "He wants to take everything from you, and since he knows he can't kill you without an endless amount of men coming after him in retaliation, he's going to ruin you publicly."

"How does he hope to do that?" I ask. "The cops have yet to track me down for the explosion, and he has no proof."

"Not enough for the cops to arrest you, but enough that there will be eyes on you and that your board has been notified of potential criminal activity."

God fucking damn it.

"So, Titan isn't trying to kill me," I repeat. "He just wants to destroy my business."

Bryson shakes his head. "No, Luc. He wants to own your business and everything else you think is yours, including his daughter."

Well, that isn't going to fucking happen. Not even over my dead body.

24

OLIVIA

Luca's been gone for hours, and he's not answering my texts. I don't know what's happening, but something tells me it's not good.

After catching up with Tori, including lots of tears, laughs, and even some more yelling, I go in search of Justine. Not only do I want Tori to meet her, but I want to know if she's heard from Jaxon, assuming he's with Luca.

"So, this Justine," Tori says skeptically. "She lives here, too?"

I nod as I press the button for her floor. "Yeah, she's been here a while. Jaxon saved her from a stalker."

I purposely leave out the part where Justine was technically forced to go with Jaxon. It's not information Tori ever needs to know about. Not until I feel confident she believes everything I've told her and not what Titan convinced her of.

"Great." Her forced word tells me we're a long way from finding a new normal within our friendship, but unfortunately, Tori doesn't have much of a choice in staying here with me.

During our earlier conversations, she explained to me what had been going on with her when we last chatted. She and her boyfriend Greg were fighting. He'd become more and more controlling, demeaning her and trying to tell her what she could and couldn't do.

Apparently, without me in the picture, the fucker thought Tori was his to command. Little does he know, when all this shit is over, he'll be getting a visit from me. Partly to put the fear of God in him if he ever tries to even look at Tori again, and also to get her things.

She didn't feel comfortable bothering Christopher—as she continues to insist on calling him—with her plight. Which is probably good, because Greg could have been used against her. With me, at least he won't be murdered. Well, not unless he gives me a good reason to do so.

I snort as we step off the elevator. Oh, how I've changed over the weeks...

Tori side-eyes me. "What's funny?"

"Just thinking about all the shenanigans the three of us are going to get into," I say with a grin. It's not far from the truth. I'm sure Justine will want to join me in threatening Tori's ex.

My best friend shakes her head and grabs my arm before we can get too far down the hallway to Justine's room. "I don't know what you're expecting from all this,

Liv. But just because I love you and I'm not running away from this place, that doesn't mean I'm staying. I wanted to talk to you about renting your mom's house if you're not going to use it."

My shoulders tense, but I force a smile to my face. "I'm sure we'll be able to figure something out, but one thing at a time, yeah?"

She smiles, but the action doesn't light up her face like it normally does. "Sure."

We get to Justine and Jaxon's room, but before my knuckles can make contact with the door, she's opening it and walking out, almost running into us.

"Oh." She glances between me and Tori. "Hi. I'm Justine." She holds her hand out.

I'm pretty sure I stop breathing until Tori accepts the gesture. "Tori. Nice to meet you."

At least she still has manners when she's upset.

Justine glances over at me. "I was just coming to see you."

"Why?" If it wasn't anything important, she could have just texted me.

"Jaxon called." My heart sinks as she says the words.

"Is Luca okay?"

Justine waves a hand in the air. "Of course. That man is indestructible. But they did get some shitty news, and they're going after Titan tonight."

Tori's gasp has us both looking at her as she says, "They can't do that."

"And why not?" I ask incredulously. "Do you not

remember everything I just told you or the pictures I showed you?"

Tori lowers her voice, and her eyes plead with me. "He's still your father, Liv. How can you just be okay with someone intent on killing him?"

I keep my head high and my words strong. "The same way he could be okay with beating the shit out of me and sending others to torture me."

She at least has the decency to look away as I say the words. Since I really don't want to end up hating Tori, I give Justine my attention. "Where are they now?"

Her eyes move between me and Tori. "Um, I'm not sure."

She's full of shit, but I understand. Why risk telling Tori anything else when there's a chance that she could still choose to believe Titan over me. The thought is disappointing, but I can't let my love for her distract me from what's important: making sure that fucker can't ever hurt anyone else again.

"Jaxon did tell me what they learned at the hospital, though," Justine adds, which has my brows rising.

"And that would be?"

She glances around the hallway and opens her door further. "We should finish this conversation in the room."

I reach for Tori's wrist, grabbing on to make sure she doesn't have any ideas about going anywhere else. "Gladly," I say, walking in with dead weight behind me.

I'll make my best friend see reason. I won't let Titan take anything else from me. Not again.

———

An hour later, I still haven't heard from Luca, but I've at least learned the whole truth right alongside Tori. It's easier for me to believe because I've seen the evil within Titan's eyes, while Tori has only seen the feigned kindness.

Still, it seems as if we're finally getting to her. There's too much that we've shared for her not to see some truth in the situation, but then again, her innocence just might be her undoing. She wants to believe the best in people, but sometimes that's just not possible.

Not when we're surrounded by wolves in sheep's clothing.

"So, what now?" Tori asks when we get back to the apartment, just the two of us.

"Now, I'm going to ask a favor of you," I say, grabbing her hand and leading her to the couch again.

She blinks at me, eyes glossy. "You're not like them."

"I'm not like my father," I correct. "I don't do bad things for personal gain, but I have changed. I told Luca that I wanted to see this through. That I want to be there when he finally has my father where he needs him in order to finish this. I know it's hard for you to believe that things like this exist in the real world when you've only heard about the bad parts and not seen them with your own eyes."

Her head drops and lip quivers. "I'm sorry I didn't trust you. I thought Luca had..."

"I know what you thought," I cut in. "And I also know you're still struggling with the truth, and that's okay. I don't hold that against you, but I need you not to hold this against me. I need to know that when I ask you to stay here, without a phone, locked in this apartment, that you'll know I'm only doing what I think is best to keep everyone safe."

"Everyone but Christopher," she says quietly.

"Yes, because he's a murdering psychopath." I don't back down from my stance, and I'm glad when she doesn't raise another argument. "I'm going to leave you in this apartment, and I promise you'll be protected here. Nobody will lay a hand on you, and when I come back, the worst will be over. We can find a new normal."

She finally looks back up at me. "Things won't ever be the same, will they?"

Even at twenty-nine years old, she's still intent on believing that there's only good in the world. If only we could all live in that reality.

I grab both of her hands and smile softly at my best friend as I shake my head. "I've changed, and I'm not sorry about who I'm becoming or who I'm doing it with."

She blushes and tries to fight a grin. "I heard what Luca said to you earlier. When you were in the bedroom."

I think back to what feels like days ago, instead of hours. He'd been commanding, telling me to be naked and talking openly about fucking me. Yeah, that attitude is one of the many things that draws me to him. I won't deny that.

"It's easy to lose myself with him," I say. "There's something satisfying about knowing how much he wants to take care of me and allowing him to command me... It's the opposite of controlling, even though it may not sound like it. Luca makes me feel freer than I have in, well, maybe ever."

Her arms reach for me, and she pulls me into a hug as she bursts into tears. "Oh, Liv. I'm so sorry."

I hold her tight and shake my head. "It's okay. Everything is going to work out. I promise."

She shudders against me, then pulls back, wiping at her cheeks. "I hope you're right."

She and I, both.

"Are you going to be okay here?" I ask, knowing that if I'm going to find Luca in time to join them, I need to go soon.

She laughs nervously. "Am I allowed to even be in this apartment when you get back?"

I forgot about finding her a room, but that doesn't matter now. Everything's changed, and I'm not kicking her out just yet.

I wink as I say, "I promise to try not to fuck Luca with you sleeping on the couch."

Her hand shoves at my shoulder. "You're terrible."

I shrug and grin. "Maybe, but you're the one who's stuck with me all these years. Yes, I've changed since I've been here, but a part of me has always been this way.

Remember that and consider why you've never left my side."

With one more hug, I get up and prepare to leave. It's time to find my father and make sure he can never come back into my life again.

25

LUCA

Learning that Titan doesn't want to kill me but wants to take everything from my grasp, all because my father left the family business to me and not him... I want to say I'm surprised, but not even close.

The more important thing is that everything makes sense now. Why he tried to get close to me and then backed off and has now conveniently been in places he shouldn't.

That all ends tonight, though. I'm done with his games. If he wanted what I had, he should have just taken it like a man instead of playing these games. Now, he's going to die an excruciating death, courtesy of the one person he wishes to destroy.

Olivia has called several times, but between moving Bryson so that Titan didn't kill him for speaking with me and making a plan of attack, I haven't had a moment to explain to her what's been going on. Instead, I allowed Justine to give her enough details, and knowing my Raven, she's going to be ready to join me.

As much as I don't want her connected to any of this, I know that if I want to keep her in my life, I can't do what I do and tell her she's not allowed to do the same.

Though, watching her own father die, no matter how big of a piece of shit he is, is something else entirely. I need to make sure that she's prepared for the mental mindfuck that will have on her. Yet, I think back to the first day I met her. The strength and resolve in her eyes and the way she handled being held captive. From entering that cell and being confined to my room, she's taken everything in stride.

I won't make the mistake of underestimating her. Not when I know in doing so, I could lose her.

She's made it very clear that she's to be there with me when I go after Titan the final time. So, no matter what I think, all I can do is tell her what to expect and ask if she's ready to face the reality of what she's asked for.

While I'm headed back to the compound to do just that, Damon and Markus are scouting out Titan's safe house. We only destroyed a third of it, so if he's hoping to bait me into any other incriminating situations, his best move would be to stay put, and I'm counting on it.

What he doesn't know, or is too cocky to consider, is that when a cop can be bought by someone, another can swoop in and up the ante. Which is what Jaxon and I have been doing since leaving Bryson in a safe house.

All of those cops Titan thought he had in his pocket have been paid triple to stand by and do nothing when they receive the call from him. Not only are they being paid triple, but I've told them I won't force their hand on anything else in the future, leaving them free to do their job with honor.

While I enjoy having my spies on the inside, I don't consider holding people hostage with their livelihoods a good business practice. Now, that's not to say I won't keep those on payroll that prefer to do dirtier business. That's something my family has done since the start.

Jaxon pulls into the compound, and I text Olivia to let her know that I'm coming up. She should be ready to go if she's as eager to do this as I've been led to believe. Her response is immediate.

My Raven: About damn time.

I smirk at her attitude. From the first meeting, she's never been afraid to speak her piece, always letting me know when she's displeased with something. With anyone else, I would have likely already put a bullet through their skull. With Olivia, it only serves to endear me.

Jaxon waits for me to walk with him toward the elevator. "Are you ready for this?"

My brows pinch together. "Of course I am."

"Not what I mean." The smirk on his face is as annoying as ever. "You're bringing your woman to a war zone. Truly subjecting her to our life and not just asking her to sneak in and out of the chaos."

I jab a finger at the call button. "Do you truly believe that Justine won't ever see you murder someone? What's the point of keeping them in our lives if we're going to hide who we truly are?"

For once, he doesn't have a smart-ass response, and before he can properly reply, the elevator doors part and there are our two women.

"Speak of the devil," I say with a grin, caused by the glare on Olivia's perfect face.

"You haven't answered your phone for me all afternoon," she says, calmer than I expect.

I move into the elevator as Jaxon does the same thing. Though, it doesn't seem as if Justine is furious with him. She wears a smirk that might be worse than Olivia's glare.

"I've been busy," I say as the doors close. "I made sure that Justine would update you through Jaxon."

"Oh, she told me," Olivia replies, then the two of them share a look that has my shoulders tensing. "And we've decided that we're both going with you."

The rumble that comes from Jaxon only serves to put a smile on my face considering the conversation we were just having.

"Not fucking happening," he says, looking only at Justine. "You have no reason to be there."

"Olivia is my friend," she says. "My only friend that I can truly be myself with. So, yes, I have a reason to be there for her and to make sure she has backup while the rest of your brutes are blowing heads off."

"She makes a point," I say as we get to the fourth floor, only Olivia and me stepping out.

The look Jaxon gives me is something I haven't seen in a long time, and I decide pushing his buttons should be something I do more often.

"We're going to our room," he says, then presses a button, shutting the doors.

Olivia looks up at me, a smile on her face. "I didn't expect you to enjoy that so much."

"Neither did I." I pick her up, wrap her legs around my waist, and start walking her toward the apartment. When she doesn't start to kiss me like I expect, I pause. "What's wrong?"

She tugs her lower lip into her mouth and looks slightly to my left. "Tori is still in there."

"I told you what would happen if you didn't find her somewhere else to sleep," I say, though I know there isn't all that much time for me to ravage her like I want. The sun has set, and plans have already been set into motion.

Olivia shoves at my chest playfully. "You wouldn't force me."

I lean forward and bite at her mouth. "No, but I'd make you really want to fuck me, regardless of who could hear, and then tell you we need to go."

Her face pales, and her lips part. "You *would* do that, you evil son of a bitch."

"You're lucky we have someplace to be, or I would fill your mouth with my cock instead of those filthy words." My darkly spoken words leave her speechless, just what I was aiming for, and I open the door into our apartment with Olivia still wrapped around me.

Sure enough, Tori is there, sitting on the couch, and her eyes widen when she sees us. I don't wave or say hello. Honestly, if I'd thought she was going to be such a pain in the ass about Titan, I might not have saved her.

That's a lie. I know it the moment I think the words. Olivia would have never been okay without her best friend, but Tori better get over whatever sentimental feelings she has toward the bastard.

He's dying tonight. No matter what anyone else thinks or wants.

Olivia waves at her. "Be right back."

Tori isn't likely considering the two of us need to change and talk, but I don't bother to say that. I carry Olivia into our room, kicking the door closed behind us, and wait to set her down until we enter the closet. As soon as she's on two feet, I start to lift up her tank top.

Her brow raises. "I thought you said we had somewhere to be?"

"We do," I confirm. "And that means you need to be dressed properly."

Once the clothing is over her head, her palms settle over my dress shirt. "So do you."

"If you're hoping to undress me, you better move faster than that, Raven."

Her hands slide down to my pants, forgetting all about my upper half, and she has them undone before I can even process what she's doing.

Olivia drops to her knees and has her sexy mouth around my cock in the next second, causing me to brace myself against the doorway of the closet. "What are you doing?"

She pulls back only long enough to answer. "Filling my dirty mouth with your cock. Sounded like fun."

This fucking vixen.

I reach one hand down, grip the back of her head, and give her everything she's just asked for. My dick drives into her mouth, hitting the back of her throat, and the choking sound she makes has me getting harder.

Her hands reach around me, and she digs her nails into my ass cheeks, taking every inch of me with renewed enthusiasm.

I'm not gentle with her, either, but that only lasts so long. If she wants part of me, then she's going to have all of me, the guest in our apartment be damned.

Once I've let her have her fun—and enjoyed the hell out of it as well—I reach for her shoulders and haul her up with one jerk. My cock slips out of her mouth with an audible pop, and the adorable pout on her face almost distracts me from yanking her pants off.

Olivia helps, wiggling them down and kicking them off with just as much urgency as I feel inside me. It isn't until I'm reaching for her again that her stare darts toward the living room. "Tori."

"Not my fucking problem," I grumble, lifting her back up and shoving my dick inside of her dripping pussy. "You are all that I care about, Raven. Everyone else can fuck right off."

As soon as I'm fully seated within her, she seems to forget all about her friend, and when I press her back against the closet wall, she rides me hard, not withholding her pleasure.

I fuck her hard and fast, fully aware that we don't have time for this if we're to get where we need to be on time, but still, I can't deny I needed this. I've craved her touch all damn day, and I'm going to savor the minutes that I give myself to escape reality with her body.

"Harder, Luc," she begs, panting heavier and gripping tightly to my shoulders as she bounces up and down.

"If I go any harder, I'm going to put you through this wall," I warn.

The smirk on her face is nearly my undoing. "You can have it fixed."

My ass clenches as I surge up into her, eliciting a gasp from between her swollen lips. I repeat the action over and over until I feel her pussy tighten around me and she squeezes her eyes closed. My hips move faster, and when I'm close, I grip the back of her neck, dragging her face closer to mine.

As I pound into her relentlessly, I own her mouth just as much as I do the rest of her body. When she can't hold back her pleasure any longer, her head jerks back and she cries out. The sound of her moans and the pulsing of her pussy have me following right behind her.

I hold her tight against me as the final waves of ecstasy roll through the both of us, but there's no time to waste. We're already going to be late.

"Go clean up, Raven," I say, pulling out of her. "You have five minutes to be dressed in jeans, boots, and a long-sleeved shirt. Nothing bulky. You'll be wearing a vest."

Both of her brows go up. "As in bulletproof vest?"

I grab her shoulders and point her body out of the closet. "Yes. Hurry the hell up or you'll be leaving here with my cum still leaking out of you."

Her mouth opens and closes, but before she can form proper words, I smack her ass, urging her to get going before I tug my shirt over my head and use it to clean her juices from my cock.

As I'm getting dressed, I realize there are raised voices coming from the living room, but it doesn't take long to figure out that it's the television turned up loudly. That has me grinning when Olivia returns to the closet.

She tilts her head to the side. "I know why you should be smiling, but I could be wrong..."

"Your friend has the TV on and turned up."

The one sentence has Olivia's entire face turning red and her eyes bouncing between me and the direction of the living room. "I can't believe I did that to her."

"You probably made her night," I say, reaching for my vest and slipping it on.

Olivia punches my stomach before it's covered. "Don't put those thoughts into my head."

Before I have to tell her again, she's pulling on clothes and moving with urgency. As she finishes getting ready, I check my phone for updates.

Damon: Just as you thought, Titan is still at his house. They have tarps up and he's going by his neighbor's houses. I assume to apologize for the earlier commotion.

Damon: He's back inside and hasn't left for more than ten minutes. Other men have shown up, all of them armed.

Damon: I've counted at least twenty men inside, but there's probably more.

Damon: Where the fuck are you?

Me: Leaving the compound in less than five.

Damon: Make sure Jaxon has the fifty-cal.

After the texts, I check my email. My chest tightens as soon as I see one at the top.

Subject: Urgent Board Meeting
Allegations have been made against our CEO and we need to discuss a plan of action before the media gets a hold of this information, which should be tomorrow according to our source.

Mr. Monroe, if you're not here for the board meeting, we will be forced to assume you're guilty of such allegations and your position will be at risk as per Article 34, Section

6.8, the board can take majority ownership of the company should the entirety be proven to be at risk.
The meeting, to happen at Monroe Investments, is set for 8:00pm tonight. Do not be late.
Signed,
Steven Griffith
Board Vice President

Fucking Titan. Bryson hadn't been exaggerating when he said that the fucker was going to target every part of my world. Worse, there's not a chance in hell that I'll make it to that meeting. Too many other things have been set into motion, which means I need a proxy and within the hour.

The only people I trust to do so are already going to be with me, which serves as another problem. I'll need to figure it out once we're in the SUV and headed to meet the others.

Olivia exits the closet dressed in dark jeans, black boots, a white long sleeve, and the vest fitted over her chest. It's not on tight, but I'll fix that once we're out of the car.

I grab her hand and pull harder than necessary, thanks to that fucking email. "We need to go."

"What's wrong?" she asks, mouth turned down into a frown.

I don't answer her as we exit the bedroom. The moment we step out, Tori turns down the TV, cheeks red.

Knowing Olivia will want a moment with her friend,

I release my hold on her. "Thirty seconds and then out that door."

I leave without waiting for her reply and text Jaxon, reminding him about the gun and hoping his insightfulness is about to save my ass again.

26

OLIVIA

It's harder than I expect it to be when I look at Tori, but I don't dare apologize for something I'm not exactly sorry for doing. I needed to fuck Luca almost as much as it seemed he needed to pound into me. Though, I do feel mildly bad for forgetting that we weren't alone.

I stand in front of Tori, and she keeps her eyes averted as I speak. "I don't know how long we'll be gone, but don't wait up."

She glances behind her. "Is it always like that?"

The grin that rises on my face can't be avoided. "Better. We were in a hurry."

"Riiight." She says the word slowly.

I glance at the open front door, then back at her. "I need to go. I love you, and please believe that we're doing the right thing."

She quiets for a beat, then asks, "When is murder ever the right thing?"

"When a man beats his daughter and plans to kill her."

I don't say anything else, nor do I wait for her reply. Instead, I turn sharply to meet Luca, closing and locking the door behind me as I go.

I thought I would feel more tension walking away from her, but when my eyes settle on Luca's back, I know I'm doing the right thing.

My fingers entwine with his, and we step into the waiting elevator. I let the doors close before I ask, "What's wrong?"

"Titan got to my board members," he says tersely.

Motherfucker. He's like the mold that just won't stop spreading. "Once he's dead, they'll have no proof of anything."

"It'll be too late," he replies. "They're holding a meeting tonight, making a decision about whatever they've been told, and if I'm not there to defend myself, I'll be removed as CEO."

My grip on his hand tightens. "They can't do that."

"They can," he murmurs. "It's written into the corporate laws of the company."

I turn toward him, shaking my head. "Why in the hell would you allow a rule like that when you know who you are?"

He doesn't answer me, and I instantly feel bad for rubbing salt in what I assume to be a gaping wound.

"Can you postpone our attack until tomorrow or later

tonight?" I ask, hoping there are options to get Luca to that meeting.

Luca shakes his head curtly as the doors open to the garage floor. "We're doing this. Now. The longer that bastard lives, the more of a risk he is to our lives. I won't let him take what's most important from me." His eyes practically burn into mine. "I can build another company. I can't replace you."

I want to say something else, but Jaxon honks the horn of the SUV, interrupting our tense moment.

Luca leads us forward, and I follow without saying anything else, since I'm not sure how much he wants to share with the others, but he barely has the door shut before he's sharing what he just told me with them.

"That son of a bitch," Justine hisses, and I decide having her with us is the best idea we had all day.

"You need a proxy," Jaxon says, staying parked even though we're supposed to be in a hurry. "Do you have one on paper or can you choose anyone?"

"It's supposed to be you," Luca replies, "but it could be anyone. Except there isn't anyone else I trust to go in my place that we don't need at the fight with us."

Jaxon's fingers drum over the steering wheel, then he looks at Justine with all the admiration in the world in his eyes. "You could do it."

I glance at Luca, expecting him to object, but surprisingly, he waits in silence.

Justine points at her chest. "Me? Like really, me?"

"Yes. You." Jaxon turns to Luca. "She could do it. She

knows enough to make this work, and she's frightening enough to keep them from trying to bully her."

My eyes bounce between the three of them, tension filling my body until I know what's going to happen.

Luca stares at Justine, whose eyes are still wide with shock. "Can you do this?"

She takes a deep breath, shoulders rising toward her ears before dropping back down. "I can. I would be honored to do this for you, Luca. You welcomed me into your home when you didn't know me. Let me help."

Her confidence grows with every word she speaks, and a smile rises to my face. I have no doubt that she'll help Luca keep his company and make those board members cower in her presence.

"Okay," he says. "Get out, wear something respectable, and take whatever car you want." He reaches for his phone again. "I'll tell them to expect you in my place."

Justine looks at me and winks. "We'll have to slay together another day."

"That we will." A soft chuckle escapes from between my lips.

She leans over to kiss Jaxon, warning him to be careful *or else*, then gets out of the SUV and rushes back to the elevator.

And just like that, one problem of the evening is solved. Here's hoping everything else goes as smoothly.

———

WITHIN TWENTY MINUTES, WE'RE PULLING UP TO the house that Luca bought earlier this week, but this time, we don't park in the garage. Jaxon backs the SUV into the driveway, next to the one I assume the others drove over in, and leaves the keys in the ignition again.

We all get out together, but Luca holds me back, standing on the porch as he pulls the front door closed. His eyes practically burn into mine. "It's not too late to back out."

My face scrunches. "What do you mean?" Hadn't he just said that this is happening tonight, right now?

"For you," he adds. "You don't have to do this with me."

I cross my arms and stare up at him with defiance written all over my face, daring him to force me to stay behind. "I'm going."

He reaches for me, holding my shoulders gently. "And I'm not saying you can't, but I want you to consider the consequences of being present when your father is killed."

"He hasn't been my father in a long time," I retort, not backing down.

"I know that, Raven, but your heart and mind might not," he says softly. "I just want to make sure that you're prepared for the mindfuck this might cause."

My head is already shaking. "I'm going to be fine, Luca. I know I've said that I hate him, which could make you think he still means something to me, but that's not it at all. What I mean when I say that is I hate *everything* he's done. The man himself means nothing to me. He is nothing, and I know that with every fiber of my being."

His hands move up my neck and cup my cheeks. "You're fucking incredible."

He kisses away my smile, but it's only seconds before he's grabbing my hand and leading us inside.

I follow without another word, but I also hope that he believes me. Seeing Titan dead will only bring me joy. I have no doubts about that whatsoever.

When we enter the house, I expect to see much of the same as I did earlier, but instead, the place has been stripped of everything left behind by its previous tenants. Dozens of men fill the empty spaces.

Some faces I recognize from being in the compound, but most of them I don't and nearly all of them I've never spoken to before. What has me most in awe is that when Luca enters the room, the murmurs quiet and all eyes go to him, full of respect.

These men are all willing to die for the man before them, and that says a hell of a lot more about Luca than it does them. It's just another reason I feel certain I've made the correct choice and that I'm right where I'm supposed to be—beside Luca.

"We only have a few minutes," Luca begins. "Some of the men are already in place around the house, but for those of you here, you'll be going in head on. We're attacking quick and dirty. Anyone still fighting beside Titan is to die except for the young man whose picture you've all been shown already."

My brow creases. I don't know who he's talking about, but it better be one of the first things he shares with me when he's done with this little speech.

"Titan is trying to take everything from us," Luca continues. "And we're going to show him what happens when someone fucks with the Monroe family. You all are part of that, and after today, we will stand stronger than we ever have. Of that I'm certain."

His hand squeezes mine, but he keeps his gaze focused on the men—and now that I'm paying more attention, even some women—before him. Cheers erupt from the crowd, and just like that, it's time for battle.

Luca is the first to step away from the group, and I follow next to him as he guides us back out the front door. The cool night air brushes over my face, and I tilt my head up to stare at the nearly full moon.

"You did good in there," I say first, and he doesn't reply. "Not that I intend on killing random people, but who is the person we're not supposed to hurt?"

He turns to me, his hands going to my vest, adjusting the straps until it's practically choking me. "It's Bryson's son."

I don't know Bryson, but this seems like it's something that's supposed to be a shock to most others. "Can I see the picture?"

Luca digs out his phone and pulls up the photo. It's more a profile view, but I get enough details to feel confident in identifying the guy. "So, if he attacks, I'm supposed to..."

"Defend yourself by whatever means necessary," he responds curtly. "I promised Bryson that I would try to keep the boy alive, but I'm not putting his life above anyone else's."

What a shitty thing to have to say to someone who was once like his family, but I don't see any other way that Luca could have handled the information or the request.

"Me and you are going in behind the others," he says once he seems confident with my vest. "I want you behind me at all times with your gun drawn."

As I'm about to ask what gun, he pulls one out from behind his back. "It's just like the one you used when Vin took you. I watched the video feed. You seemed confident with it."

It's not a question, but I can see the worry in his eyes, so I nod. "I had some practice as a teen, and I'm not scared of pulling the trigger."

That's the best I can offer him, and I hope it's enough not to have him changing his mind. When he closes his eyes longer than necessary to blink and takes a heavy breath, I know I'm not going to like his next words.

"We should have focused more on training you," he says, then glances behind us as others have already exited from the house. "I believe that you want to be here, but I shouldn't let you do this. It's more risk than I'm willing to take with your life."

He isn't actually telling me that I need to stay behind, which I appreciate, but I also don't need to be a distraction for him. Maybe there's a happy medium we can agree on, considering I'm really only here to make sure Titan is dead by the end of the night. After all, it's not as if I have a death wish.

"What if we compromise and I stay two houses down and only enter the house once the initial burst of bullets have passed," I suggest, then add, "You can wait for me by the front door, and I'll wait for you to text 'go' or something."

His hands cup both my cheeks, and he presses his forehead against mine as he speaks. "I think you just might be the best thing that has, and will ever, happen to me, Olivia Danes."

"Of course I am." I grin widely. "I take it that you like my offer?"

"It will allow me to be more focused," he says, pulling back. "So, yes. You stay hidden, and I promise to bring you in as soon as it's safe."

That's not exactly what I said, but I let it go. If I have to, I'll go in without him. I won't miss my chance to make sure Titan knows he truly means nothing to me. I want him to know that he hurt me before, but that he can't ever do so again. Not only because he'll be dead, but because any attachments I had to him as a child have been completely severed.

Luca gives me another quick kiss that I try to savor as long as appropriate. After being unsure if he'd ever be ready to press his lips to mine, I won't ever take these moments for granted.

"I need to go," he says, voice deep and filled with more emotions than we have time to process right now.

"Be safe. I'll see you soon," I reply, squeezing both his hands before pushing him toward a waiting Jaxon and Markus. "I'll be ready and waiting."

At least for a little while.

27

LUCA

Leaving Olivia behind isn't something I'd normally feel comfortable with, but twice in one day and at the same house, I've been left with no other options. Well, besides having forced her to stay home.

I would have done so if we'd been going after anyone other than her father. But we aren't, so here I am, walking away from her and hoping I'm not making the biggest mistake of my life. Though, after hearing the conviction in her words about needing to be here, I don't worry as much as I had been.

Jaxon and Markus are joining me in leading the other group inside now that we don't have Olivia to worry about. Damon is around the back side of the house with a smaller group, and with timed precision, we march forward.

Though, this is nothing like earlier. As soon as we step foot into the yard, bullets come flying at us, so it's time to run, ducking and dodging as best we can to avoid being hit.

It's to our advantage to have the bigger group moving and evading, but that only lasts until we get to the front. Half of the group breaks down the plywood that was added to cover the gaping hole from the explosion. The other half goes with me through the front door, which is locked.

Since my leg still isn't at its best, Jaxon steps forward and kicks it in within three tries but takes a bullet to the chest.

He sucks in a breath and moves behind me, waving everyone else forward. The vest stopped the bullet from actually penetrating him, but that doesn't mean the impact doesn't hurt like a son of a bitch.

I go ahead, gun raised and ready to shoot without question, except once again, Titan is more prepared than I expect. Rows of men line every open space within the house. All of them are armed and shooting at us.

A bullet hits me in the lower middle of my vest, and another grazes my bicep, leaving blood running down my arm. Thank fuck Olivia stayed behind, because this is going to be messy.

I fire back, taking down a man with every bullet that leaves my gun. Still, the men next to me aren't as lucky. While plenty of Titan's men lie dead, so do several of mine.

We continue to push forward, leaving behind our

brothers and sister to be taken care of later. It's the harsh reality of our lifestyle, and we will grieve them later.

My left arm burns from the wound, but I don't stop shooting except when I have to replace my mag. Shouts and cries echo through the house, and the smell of blood and gunpowder is heavy in the air, but I don't let any of that distract me as I continue to take life after life.

My eyes don't stop searching for Titan, though. Unless he has more underground tunnels, the rat is here somewhere, likely calling for help that will never come. Even the neighbors' concerns will go unanswered until we're done here.

Only then will the police come and clean up our mess. Not a moment sooner.

Jaxon is back to standing upright, but he's bleeding from his side and there's a pinched expression on his face. I grab his arm and push back. "Get the fuck out of here." My eyes glance down to his wound. "That's too much blood."

He jerks out of my hold and sneers at me. "I'm not leaving until you do."

Stubborn fucking prick strides back to the front line and keeps shooting. I should force him out of the house, but I would be the same way. We both know that if it's our time to die, this is the only way we'd want to go out.

Protecting our family.

A glimpse of something catches my attention, but by the time I move my focus, it's gone. I slip behind a wall, moving toward the hallway, and see what I hope is the same shadow.

Someone is on the move, and they're doing their best not to be seen.

There are more of my men down this hallway than there are Titan's, so I push forward, gesturing for some of them to head back toward the front of the house where the numbers aren't as even. I continue past them, though. My gut tells me that Titan is the shadow, and if he's not, it's someone who will know where he is.

As I pass by Bryson's old room, I see a body being dragged out. It's his son. One of my men is pulling him by the arms, the young man's limp body hitting every bit of rubble on the way out. He's going to feel like shit later, but at least he'll be alive. Or so I assume.

Continuing on, I get to a stairwell and start to go up. None of the lights are on up here, and when I find a switch, it doesn't work. Great. Night vision wasn't something I intended on needing.

A bullet whizzes past my head, nearly taking me out. I stay quiet and lower myself to the ground, unsure if the shooter can see me when I can't see them. Either way, I'm not backing down. This must end tonight.

I race up the stairs, knowing that the longer I stay in the dark, the more of a target I am. I'm almost to the top when a bullet hits my gut, the vest protecting me from bleeding out, but I still fall to my knees. Agony pulses through my body. A shot that close still does considerable damage, even with the added protection.

When my eyes close and see Olivia's face, I know I need to push through whatever inner torment I have and get my ass to the second floor. She needs me to find Titan, and that's what I'm going to do. No matter what it costs me, as long as it's not her, I will end him.

Now that I'm closer to the top, I can hear the breathing of whoever is waiting for me up top, and my plan changes. I thump my head against the nearest stair and groan as if I've truly been shot, not making a move to get up.

It's a risk to lay here, but considering what I know about Titan, I believe that if he has the chance to see me suffer, he's not going to miss the opportunity.

I roll to my back and use the blood from my arm where I was shot earlier to rub on my stomach, hoping it will have them believing I'm more seriously injured. Just as I smear the crimson over the spot beneath my vest, someone steps onto the stairs.

"He's bleeding," the voice says, quiet yet firmly.

"Bring him to me."

Mother fucking bingo.

I knew Titan wouldn't be able to pass up the opportunity to rub his victory in my face, which I eagerly await just so I can prove him wrong.

Allowing myself to be dragged by my vest up the stairs and tossed onto the floor isn't my finest moment. It takes every ounce of self-control for me to not fight back, but the moment I see Titan sitting there in the black wingback chair placed within the middle of a secondary living area and with his smug smile, I know I've made the right move.

It's only him and the one who brought me up. There's no one else to protect him. He's sent everyone else downstairs. What a fucking idiot.

He places his hands on the velvet armrests and pushes himself up and out of the chair. He's dressed in a dark silver suit, white dress shirt, and no tie, trying to be someone he's never been.

Titan stands over me as the other guy, dressed more like me and prepared to fight, removes the weapons I carry. Well, almost all of them.

With me on my back, he misses the knife I have there. It's the one I always carry with me into a fight and hasn't ever let me down. Let's hope today is no different.

"All these years, and you had no clue who I was," Titan begins, the smug look on his face grating on my nerves. "Your father was like a brother to me. I loved him and even you when you were a boy, but I'd been forgotten, cast aside. As if all the sacrifices I'd made over the years meant nothing."

His eyes darken as he bends closer, lifting me up by my vest. "That wasn't something I could let your father get away with."

"So, you're punishing me for his mistakes?" I ask, forcing my voice to sound weaker than I am.

He chuckles and shoves me back to the ground before standing again. "No, I'm ruining you just like you ruined me."

"I didn't even know who—"

His boot slams into my stomach where he assumes I've been shot. Though the fact that there isn't more blood seeping from the wound should give me away, his anger seems to be distracting him from his common sense.

"I gave up everything," he roars. "I left my family to come claim what was mine, to make a better life for them, and even though I still risked my life for *him*, nobody was there for me when I needed them. Your father first, and then you. He paid for that mistake with his life, and now you're going to find the same fate as him."

I know that Bryson said Titan hadn't killed my dad himself, but hearing him take claim for his death, no matter how cruel my father had been in raising me, I know I can't lay here and do nothing. Not any longer.

Reaching for the knife still behind my back, I lean forward and aim for the silent guard, sending the sharp blade through his chest in the next second. He teeters briefly, and I worry that the single weapon isn't going to do the job, but he finally drops to his knees, holding his chest, before falling onto his face.

I'm on my feet, still sore as fuck from having been shot, even if not all the bullets penetrated my skin, but I need Titan to die. I scramble for the guard's gun, but by the time I'm turned around, Titan has already drawn his own.

Pointing the weapon at my head, he says, "I wouldn't do that if I were you."

"Why? You're nothing to me," I say with venom, not forgetting that I need to incapacitate this piece of shit so I can call for Olivia. "Just a pathetic man who has spent his whole life trying to be someone he never could be."

The hate he throws my way with his eyes lets me know I've said just the right thing, but as I'm about to take advantage of his distracted rage, he says the one thing that could save his life. At least for the moment.

"I have Olivia."

With my borrowed pistol still pointing at him, I glance around, but she's nowhere to be seen. "Bullshit."

"Kill me and see just how much 'bullshit' you find," he taunts.

Fucking hell. I don't know how the man is always a step ahead of me, but the moment I finally get to take his life will be one of the greatest days of mine.

"What do you want?" I ask with more regret than I've ever felt.

28

OLIVIA

The cacophony of gunfire and screams are making me anxious, but I've stayed put as I promised Luca. Though, I don't know how much longer I can stay here.

Men are dragged from the house, and I assume most or all of them are dead. Bullets mar the fence nearest to me, having come through the broken-out windows. Neighbors peek out their windows, phones up to their ears, but I have a feeling help won't be arriving anytime soon.

The gun Luca left with me stays in my hands at all times as I keep my eyes moving around. I wouldn't think anyone would expect me to be out here, but I refuse to lower my guard, not when this moment feels so monumental. It's all or nothing tonight.

We win or we lose. There is no in between. No

regrouping to return at a later date. Titan has done too much damage not to end him now.

My phone buzzes with a text that I hope like hell is from Luca.

Justine: This isn't good. The board let me speak on Luca's behalf and I know I made a few of them see reason, but they kicked me out while they put things to a vote. I don't know if it was enough.

Fuck. I know Luca said he didn't care if he lost his company, that he could build another, but I don't want this for him. He's worked too damn hard to protect all he's built, providing just enough good in his fucked-up world that I know he doesn't deserve what Titan's done to him.

Resting the phone over the pistol in one hand, I use the other and start to type out a response to Justine, needing her to know that no matter what happens, the fact that she tried is more than appreciated. Except before I can finish the sentence, a palm covers my mouth, and a blade goes to my neck.

"Drop the phone and gun," the grumbly voice demands.

I consider my options. If I don't listen, I might be able to shoot him, but will he slit my throat in the process? The possibility is high. Still, dying might be better than being held captive by Titan again, allowing him the satisfaction of killing me himself.

"We have Luca," he adds. "If you want to say your goodbyes, I'd suggest doing as you're told."

Mother fuck fuck.

I never should have let him go into that house without me. I thought I was making the right choice, staying behind so that he wouldn't be distracted, but clearly that didn't help shit.

"Fine." I release the pistol and phone, holding my hands up. "Care to remove the knife from my neck now?"

"No, actually I wouldn't," he retorts. "I saw what you did to Bryson. Titan almost didn't let him go to the hospital, and he likes him."

I can't see his face, but that doesn't mean I don't hear the annoyance in his voice. "Why work for someone who doesn't appreciate you?"

He shoves me forward. "Walk."

"Do you always do other people's dirty work without knowing if you'll die for nothing?" I press, since he avoided my first question.

The knife presses further into my skin, drawing blood. "Shut the fuck up before I *accidentally* kill you."

His sinister voice has me doing as he says, watching my surroundings as he guides me around the back side of the house, through a door where there isn't anyone else that I can see. The blade is pulled from my neck as he pushes me toward a set of stairs, knocking me down. "Walk."

Not a fucking chance in hell.

I turn over like I'm going to get up, but I brace myself

on my elbows and pull my right leg back before pushing it forward with every ounce of strength I can muster.

The sole of my boot connects with his groin, forcing him to hunch over, gasping for air. I stand and rush for him just as I hear the sound of gunshots much closer than the rest. While I don't let myself get distracted, my attacker is stronger than I anticipate.

As soon as I reach for the knife still clutched in his hand, he arcs his arm and drives the tip of the blade into my thigh.

"You're fucking lucky he prefers you alive," he says, leaning closer with his face only inches from mine.

His pale skin and blue eyes hold little life in them, and the scars covering his skin make me wonder if he works for Titan, uncaring about respect because he has a death wish.

His fingers tangle with my hair, lifting me back to my feet by the strands as he snarls. "Stand and walk. Now."

With the searing pain expanding through my leg, I do as he says, but with considerably more effort. "Where are you taking me?"

His chuckled breath moves over the back of my ear as he puts the knife back to my neck, staying only half a step behind me. "After the gunshots I just heard, hopefully to see the dead body of your boyfriend."

I suck in a shuddering breath. I want to believe he's wrong, that Luca couldn't be so easily defeated, but there's a fear inside me that grows stronger by the second, increasing my motivation to get upstairs.

I say nothing else. No more trying to reason with the deranged man behind me, no more hoping that this night isn't going to end without considerable loss, some I may not be prepared to process.

When we're finally at the top, he shoves me against the wall and turns me before we can see around the corner. "If you don't want your vocal cords cut out, you won't say a fucking word unless spoken to. Not even a gasp. Do you understand?"

More blood leaks from what I hope is the same place he cut me before. I want to nod instead of speak, but I'm afraid to move my head.

"Yes," I whisper so as not to make my throat move more than necessary.

The sinister grin on his face makes my stomach churn, and I hope like hell he's dead sooner rather than later. Though, with my current position, I'm not sure how that's going to happen.

He turns me back around, and when we step onto the landing, he wraps an arm around my waist, holding me close as if he's using my body as a shield against whatever we're about to find up here.

I close my eyes briefly, preparing myself for the chance that Luca's lifeless body could be on the ground, but when I open them back up, I see his back and Titan in front of him, holding a gun.

A situation nearly as bad as Luca being dead.

"And there's our guest of honor," Titan says joyfully. "Come here, Daughter."

I don't make a move to go to him. I have zero desire to stand by his side, but when the fucker behind me digs the knife into my side this time, encouraging me forward, I know I have no choice but to listen.

While not great, there's still a chance Luca and I can make it out of this situation, together and alive. I'll do whatever I'm forced to if it means increasing those odds.

The man behind me never leaves his position, even when I'm standing next to Titan as requested. My eyes meet Luca's, and the relief at knowing he's not dead increases the hope I have within me that we'll survive this. Somehow.

Titan skims the tips of his fingers over my jaw. "You've turned out better than I could have dreamed." The reverence in his voice nearly makes me gag considering he wanted to kill me a week ago. "Please tell me that you've reconsidered my offer and you'll join me."

"As what?" I ask, though my eyes never leave Luca's hardened stare. "Your daughter, someone you respect, or your prisoner, someone you still intend to kill?"

I have no desire to join Titan in any shape or form, but I need time for Luca to snap out of whatever rage-filled stupor he's in and make a fucking move.

"As my daughter, of course," Titan coos, but I don't for one second believe him, just like I didn't before. He only wants me so Luca can't have me. If my father had truly yearned for me, he'd have returned long before I got swept up in all this.

"I made a mistake before, not taking better care of

you. I blame it on only having just found out your mother died." He has the audacity to just now tear up. "She would have wanted us to be a family again. It's all she ever talked about when we spoke."

God, his lies make me want to throw up. There's no fucking way he's telling the truth or even gives a damn about my mother, but still, I indulge him.

"You kept in touch?" I blink at him with feigned sorrow. There's no way they kept in touch. Not in recent years, at least. She rarely even uttered his name over the last five years, the pictures of him all removed from the house as if he never existed.

I'm rather sure she hated him.

He nods, stepping closer to me. "Even if I couldn't be part of your life, Olivia, I never forgot about either of you."

Yet, he hadn't known she was dead when he first captured me. He's lying. He's using the love I hold for my mother against me. Fucking vile excuse of a human being.

Though, two can play that game.

"I always wondered why she never moved on," I muse, my gaze flickering down to my feet. "She didn't have to."

"No, I was still her husband as much as I could be, and now I want to be your father again," he says so lovingly that I nearly vomit. "Let me make up for our past."

Like when you tried to kill me, I think but don't utter.

Instead, I glance at Luca and see the life returning to

him. His eyes are locked on me, and I ever so slightly nod at him. He's in a better position to make a move than I am, even though I'm closer. He still has his gun, although he's kept it lowered. He can shoot Titan. End this nightmare.

Except he shakes his head, his eyes moving briefly to the man behind me.

Luca doesn't want me to get hurt.

Well, too fucking bad. He's going to have to get over that fact or we're both going to be dead, because I can't pretend to even like Titan, let alone want to stand by his side, for much longer.

I turn to Titan, but I'm really speaking to Luca. "Why don't you start by killing the man who made me bleed?"

The knife the man behind me wields hasn't moved far from my ribs, ready to puncture a lung or kidney within a moment's notice. But if Luca shot him, even in the arm, it would allow me to back away instead of being a human shield.

Titan shakes his head. "Trust is a fickle thing, dear daughter. As much as I want us to be a family, you still have to earn your place. You did run away from me last time."

"And you beat the shit out of me, so I'd say we're even." My words come out sweetly, and I even manage to smile at him. Though, a part of me hopes he can see the hate in my eyes and know that he's nothing to me any longer and never will be. "But I can rebuild trust, Dad.

Just as I know you can. If Mom still believed in you, then I'm sure we can find a way to work things out. To be a family."

I circle the conversation back, needing Titan to feel as though he's won. He needs to think he's taken Luca's company, infiltrated his family, and now taken the woman he cares most about. Only then will we see Titan's true colors.

My stare goes back to Luca, and I glare at him, using the hate I have toward Titan to keep my ruse up. "Can we kill him now? He's put my life in danger long enough."

Titan's fingers wrap around my shoulder, and he brings his face closer to mine. "We can, but are you sure you want to see this?"

Still looking at Luca, I nod. "More than anything else. Even if I have to hurt in the process. I just want this done. Now."

Luca blinks twice, and I hope it's in understanding of what I'm saying and that he doesn't believe a single word spoken merely as a distraction for Titan.

Seconds tick by and I wait, my heart hammering in my chest and hands shaking. It's now or never. We're running out of time.

Finally, I see him move his arm behind his back, doing something with the gun I saw, and I hope like hell that I know what's coming next. He has to fucking shoot *someone*. I have no clue if it will be the man behind me or Titan. I'm not terribly concerned with which happens first, but either way, there's a chance that I'm about to be shot or stabbed.

My body tenses for either one, and when the first bullet is fired, my eyes shoot open and I cry out. Not only is my arm grazed, but the blade cuts through my shirt, using the opening in the vest to stab me.

"Fuck!" I grip my side and drop to the ground, then everything happens too quickly for me to process. Nothing is thought through. Only actions spur my movements as I hear two more gunshots echo around us.

My adrenaline and will to survive keep me moving. I take the knife from my side, ripping it out of me, and just as Titan raises his gun at Luca, I slice at his wrist, rendering his shooting arm useless.

He howls in pain and tries to kick me, but I roll out of the way and get to my feet. Luca is beside me now, but I pay him no attention, not even when he reaches for my bleeding arm.

Instead, my sights are on Titan. The man whose DNA runs through me, who I used to look up to as a little girl, begged to push me higher on our swing set in the backyard, and hoped I could be as strong as when I grew up.

So much admiration that I used to hold for him. Admiration that turned to pain when he disappeared, and I was left without a father. Now, it's a resolve mixed with the drive to no longer have to worry about ever seeing his face again. I need to know that he'll never hurt me or anyone else again because he no longer exists in the world.

A strong desire for him to just be gone encompasses my whole being.

"Are you sure, Raven?" Luca asks quietly. "Really sure?"

He must see the intent in my gaze as I step forward. "He's mine."

Even though I've never killed anyone, there isn't a part of me that's afraid of what I'm about to do. This is why I knew I needed to be here. Deep down, it wasn't just about me watching Titan die; I wanted to be the one to take his life. A payment for all the pain he caused me and my mother, then and now.

Titan presses himself against the wall behind him, his sneer on me. "You won't kill your own father. I raised you better than that."

I chuckle darkly. "You didn't raise me. Mom did, and she taught me to always be responsible for my own problems." I point the knife at his face. "This is me making her proud."

He moves to strike me, but Luca catches his fist before any contact can be made. I open my mouth to stop Luca from taking over the situation, but he surprises me when all he does is pin Titan's arms behind his back.

Titan struggles against Luca's hold, face turning red with indignation as if he can't believe his years of scheming have come down to this moment, facing his own daughter who wishes for nothing more than his death. Though, a little torture inflicted upon him might make things more interesting.

At least, that's what I hope until he starts to speak again.

"Your whore of a mother wouldn't be pro—" Whatever idiocy he's about to say is cut off when I slice the knife across his throat. It's brutal and intimate—up close and personal and done without a second thought or regret.

A fitting ending that has me smiling as he gurgles, blood oozing from his throat and coloring his pristine suit with crimson.

Luca releases him, and he drops to his knees, kneeling at my feet and staring up at me with shock. His fingers move to cover the wound, but it's too late. Titan won't survive this, and I watch gleefully every second as the life fades from his eyes.

"You should have stayed dead," is all I have left to say to him before he falls onto his side, the final twitches of death moving through him.

Luca is at my side in the next second, but the frown on his face is the last thing I expect. He isn't saying anything. He's just looking at me, searching my face for something I'm not sure he'll ever find there again.

He told me before that my innocence drew him to me, that there was a light inside me that called to him unlike anything ever had before.

Does he not see me as someone worthy any longer now that I've killed my own father? If so, do I care?

Not even a second after the thought enters my mind, I know I don't. I'm not ashamed of who I've become since meeting Luca. The strength I've acquired and the fight for survival...all of it has brought me to this moment, and this isn't anything I have to regret.

"If you can't—" I start to tell him that if he can't handle what I've done, then he can fuck right off, but he kisses the words away, holding my cheeks almost painfully tight.

I kiss him back, ignoring the blood dripping from various parts of both our bodies and reveling in the fact that the worst is over. We won. Titan can't ever hurt us or anyone we care about again.

Luca slows the kiss down and pulls back just far enough to look into my eyes. "You're more than I could have ever dreamed of. The other half of me that I didn't know was missing until I met you, and I'm going to spend the rest of my life showing you how fucking worthy of love you are."

Covered in blood, surrounded by three dead bodies, and this man basically tells me he loves me for the first time. All I can do is smile and lightly laugh, because this is my life now and I don't think I could be any happier about that.

"I'm glad to know romance isn't dead, even in the mafia," I joke, pushing up onto my toes to kiss him again.

Before I can, he smirks. "Just those guys," he says, making me laugh even harder. Fuck, if I don't want him to take me right here, amongst all the chaos.

Though, instead of furthering our kiss, he pulls back and looks my body over. "We need to get you taken care of."

As the adrenaline wears off and the aches within my barely healed body start to surface, I know he's not wrong. Plus, I'm sure there is only so much time we can spend here without the cops finally needing to show up. I can ravage him later, when we're home and properly celebrating.

I slip my hand into his and nod. "Let's go home."

"Nothing has ever sounded more perfect."

29

LUCA

Watching Olivia kill Titan, seeing the satisfaction in her eyes as she took his life, is the moment I could finally admit to myself that I love her. Nothing in this world could ever get between us. It's me and her against the world.

She is everything I didn't know I needed, but now that I do, I'm never going to let her go. Not for anything or anyone. Not only would I burn the world for this woman, but I would die for her without a second thought.

My Raven has stripped away all the barriers my father instilled in me. She has made me see that loving someone isn't the curse he made it out to be when he continually kept me at arm's length, treating me more as one of his new recruits than his own son until I was old enough to kill. I'd been stripped of all emotion, caving to his desires.

We're both a mess, but the night isn't over yet. The

gunfire has ceased below us, and when we're halfway down the stairs, Jaxon is limping around the corner.

The relief on his face when he sees both of us is a reminder of how lucky I am to have him in my life, even when he drives me fucking crazy.

"You two look like you've been better," he says, then coughs roughly, spitting up a bit of blood.

"So do you," I reply, giving him a onceover. "Seems like we're going to be keeping Dr. Theo quite busy tonight."

"I already called him." Jaxon grimaces. "Markus is driving Damon back to the compound now."

I tense, not prepared for bad news even if I expect it, given the firepower that was exchanged here tonight.

"What happened?" Olivia asks for me when I can't find the words.

"D took a bullet to the gut," Jaxon replies with a frown. "There was a fuck-ton of blood."

"And the others?" I ask, finally finding my words.

Jaxon glances behind him and shrugs. "Not sure yet, but it isn't good. Some of these men will need to go to the hospital. Theo can't treat everyone in time."

"Send them," I say. "We have the cops on our side for the night. We'll handle everything needed to prevent this from getting out of hand."

He nods, and the three of us move through the hallway together. Bodies litter the floor, but I don't avert my stare. Some of these men were my family, my responsibility. They died for me, and I won't pretend otherwise, even if I barely knew their names.

I see Liam, Aiden, and Caleb among the first group of fallen, three brothers who had lost their parents to a robbery gone wrong and wound up at my doorstep, looking for help with their vengeance.

Further into the house, there are more, nearly a dozen that I can identify and likely more that I can't. It's going to be a long fucking day of brutal phone calls. I may not have known any of them well, but they made a commitment to my family and I did the same to theirs.

Each of them will get a personal call from me, along with a payment that will mean nothing in the grand scheme of things, but maybe it will relieve some of the stress while they grieve.

Olivia's grip on my hand grows looser, and she starts to wobble. "Whoa," she says, trying and failing to hold on to me. "I think I need to sit for a minute."

"I think you need to be stitched up before you lose any more blood," I say, then turn to Jaxon, but he speaks before I need to.

"I'll finish here," he says. "Take care of your girl."

His comment reminds me that *his girl* was also doing something important while we were here, but that's the least of my worries as Olivia's skin grows paler.

I pick her up and see that the SUV has already been brought up from the other house. I sit Olivia in the passenger's seat and lean it back before buckling her in.

Her head lolls to the side, and I slam the door shut before running to the other side of the SUV.

I'm tempted to take her straight to the hospital instead, but my phone vibrates with a text, changing my mind.

Markus: Damon is stitched up and the doc has done everything he can. The rest is up to D. Theo has blood for every type ready and waiting for anyone else. He can only handle five more, though.

Me: Bringing Olivia home. She might need blood.

I hit the gas and drive like her life depends on it, because I'm fairly certain that it does. While home is further away than the nearest hospital, Theo won't ask questions that waste precious time, and I feel confident he'll take better care of her than anyone else.

When I pull into the garage, Theo and Markus are waiting there for us. That doesn't give me much hope for Damon that they've left him alone, but I can't worry about him right now when Olivia hasn't said a word to me the entire way back.

"She's unconscious," I snap when Markus opens the door.

Theo has a stretcher with supplies on it, and I don't get to the other side fast enough to help them move her. She's on the stretcher, and I reach for her hand, squeezing her cold fingers. "Fight, Raven."

She's done so for weeks. I know she can for one more night. After tonight, she can rest all she needs. Nobody will ever hurt her again. I just need her to fight a little longer.

Markus pushes her into the elevator while Theo checks over her wounds. "She was stabbed and cut several times." He looks closer at her upper arm. "Well, this one might be from a bullet."

"No fucking shit," I sneer, then take a deep breath. "Anything vital?"

"Not that I can see, but the blood loss is a problem," he answers, prepping her for an IV as soon as we're still, waiting on the elevator to take us upstairs. "It'll be a bit before I can tell you anything more than that."

I want to scream into the sky. This can't be real. We just won. She was smiling and even laughing. What in the fuck is actually happening right now?

The doors open, and I stand aside, too pent-up to move, but when I hear Tori's screech from inside the apartment, something in me snaps.

I rush into the living room and glare at her. One look is all it takes to have her backing up.

"What can I do?" I ask Theo as he begins to stitch Olivia up and the drip for more blood starts, replacing the blood she's still losing.

"Hold this." He hands me tape, then begins stitching her wounds with a needle. He places gauze over the first cut. "Tape."

I rip two pieces, watching helplessly as he quickly moves on to the next injury.

She starts to groan, and he takes the tape from me. "If you can get her to wake up, that's good."

Without needing to be told twice, I'm standing next to her head and stroking her face. "Raven? Can you hear me?"

She opens her mouth, but no words come out.

"You don't have to speak," I say. "Just open those beautiful blue eyes."

Her head falls to the side, but I grab her cheeks. "Olivia, listen to me. You need to stay awake. You need to fight. I can't..."

I let the words trail off, because losing her now, after everything we've been through together since meeting, isn't fucking possible. I refuse to believe it's even an option. She's going to be okay. Whatever is going on inside her body, she's going to fight to live like she's done so many times before.

"Please," I beg her quietly, watching her face for any further signs of movement.

Just when I'm about to release her, her eyelids flutter and I call out her name again. She blinks several times before her eyes stay open, and I want to weep with relief.

"Thank fuck," I murmur, pressing my lips lightly to her forehead. "Stay with me, Raven."

She mumbles something I can't understand, but she isn't moaning in pain or closing her eyes, so I continue to speak to her.

"We're back at the apartment," I say. "Theo is working on you. Probably the only other man on Earth that's allowed to touch you without fear of losing his hands." I chuckle at myself, feeling the need to keep things light for her sake. "Markus and Damon are back, too. Jaxon is still getting men out of the house, or he's on his way back. I'm not sure—"

"Olivia!" Justine's voice screeches through the apartment, and I cut a glare at her.

"Be fucking quiet."

She covers her mouth and nods, then joins Olivia at her other side. I catch Tori out of the corner of my eye and sigh. Olivia probably wouldn't mind seeing her, either, much to my dismay.

As soon as I gesture with my head for Tori to join Justine, she does, tears tracking down her cheeks as she quietly sobs, covering her mouth with one hand.

"She's going to be okay," I say out loud. Though, I'm not sure whose benefit the words are for.

The three of us hover around her while Theo finishes stitching her up and then increases the flow of her transfusion. He removes his bloody gloves and gives her another onceover.

"She should be okay," he says. "Even if she isn't talking yet, the fact that she's remaining moderately conscious leaves me optimistic. I'll give her some meds for the pain, which will dull the shock of everything, and she should be more talkative."

I grip his forearm, dirtying his white dress shirt. "Thank you, Theo."

He nods, his appreciation for my gratitude showing through his eyes and smile. "You're welcome, Luca."

He goes to check on Damon again, and I know I should do the same, but I can't stand the thought of leaving Olivia's side. The thought of having her close her eyes only to never open them again and me not being the last person she sees...

When Theo returns a few minutes later, he injects what I assume are the meds he was just speaking of into her arm, and all the rest of us can do is wait.

Justine glances up at me, tears in her eyes. "Why isn't Jaxon here, Luc?"

Fuck. I'm such an asshole. I would have thought he called her already.

"He's fine," I say hurriedly. "He should be back soon."

At least, I fucking hope so. I thought Olivia was fine and then she wasn't, but I don't voice that thought to Justine. She doesn't need that right now. None of us do.

Her shoulders drop, and she closes her eyes, head tilted to the sky. "Thank you." When she looks at me again, she smiles triumphantly. "Oh, and I won."

I have no clue what she's talking about, so I don't respond, but she elaborates.

"Your company," she adds. "It's still yours."

That's the last thing on my mind right now, but I

can't deny her words loosen a bit of the tension in my chest. "Thank you."

She nods, but before any of us can say anything else, Olivia speaks.

"This fucking sucks," she mutters. All of the words sound jumbled together, but still, they make the rest of us smile, then she looks at me. "I didn't dream that. He's really dead."

I stroke her face gingerly. "Yes, Raven. He'll never hurt you again. You're safe."

Her eyes close, but she's smiling, and I let her have this moment of peace in silence. She killed her own father. I thought she'd be traumatized by the action, but if she wants to be happy, then I won't stand in her way.

Though, I look at Tori again, whose tears have finally ceased. I swear if she tries to make Olivia feel at all guilty...I won't be responsible for what I do.

When Olivia opens her eyes again, she glances around at the three of us and sighs. "We're going to be okay."

"We are," I promise and rub my thumb over the back of her hand. "Nobody will ever hurt you again."

I'd said it before, yet here we are again, with her in a hospital bed. But this time, I'll do whatever it takes to make sure there is never another reason for anyone to want to harm a hair on her head.

Even if she's strong enough to fight her own battles as she showed today, I'd rather never feel this way again.

EPILOGUE
OLIVIA

Today is the first day that I've woken up without a bruise or open wound on my body in what feels like forever. Four weeks have passed since the day I killed my father, and every day since has been better than the last.

While I haven't done much as I've focused on healing, knowing that nobody else is coming after us—at least for the time being—has given me a joy I didn't know I needed in my life. Much like Luca.

Luca has watched over me constantly. He doesn't like to leave my side for long, as if he expects me to fall apart at a moment's notice, and while some days he drives me crazy, I appreciate the love he's shown me.

Maybe one day I'll have regrets about slicing my father's throat open, but I haven't had a single nightmare, so I'm not holding my breath.

Though, I also won't complain about no longer

feeling the need to murder anyone. Not now that the people who did me harm are all dead. Aside from Bryson, but he gets a pass since he helped me escape.

Plus, he didn't stick around. He took his son and left the day after the battle. Nobody knows where they went, but Luca suspects we'll see them again one day.

As I attempt to roll out of bed, Luca's arm wraps around me, stopping my movements. "Where do you think you're going?" he grumbles.

"To the shower," I reply sweetly. "Care to join me before I leave for breakfast and shopping with Justine and Tori?"

His head lifts quickly from his pillow. "You're leaving the compound so soon?"

I lean over and cup his cheek. "Luca, love. It's been weeks. I'm healed, and Theo cleared me days ago to resume all regular activity. You can't fuck me like you did last night—twice—and then tell me I'm not well enough to leave the house."

He pushes me onto my back and moves to press his body over mine, managing to line his morning wood up perfectly with my floozy of a pussy. "I bet I could fuck you into staying."

There's a real possibility that he could, but Justine already warned me that she would drag my naked ass out of this room if I wasn't downstairs by ten this morning. It's already nine. We slept in later this morning than our normal, but being fucked on the dinner table and then again in the bedroom took considerable energy and had us up much later than normal.

His hips press forward, and he smirks. "You're thinking about it."

I shove him off me. "I was thinking about last night. If you want round three, you're going to have to get a quicky in the shower or risk Justine walking in on us."

Luca tries to reach for me again, but I manage to slide off the bed before he can grab my arm. Though, I don't even make it around the bed before he's out and entering the bathroom first.

Apparently, I get shower sex before brunch with my best friends. An incredible start to the day that I can't at all complain about.

He turns on the water, and since we're both already naked, he presses me against the glass. I gasp from the cool temperature, but his mouth eats up the sound as he grips the back of my neck, tilting my head until he finds the angle he's looking for.

My hands are clawing at his chest, already eager for his cock even though it's been less than eight hours since I had all of him.

His hand slips between my legs and he presses two fingers against my clit, causing my hips to jolt forward of their own accord.

The cocky grin on his face is the most precious thing I've ever seen, but I don't get to enjoy it long before he's guiding me into the tile shower and bending me over. "Hands on the wall, Raven."

I do as he says, happily sticking my ass out for him as water sprays over my back. His palm smacks over my left cheek, then the right, rubbing the sting out of each one before he trails his fingers down my ass to my pussy.

"Always so ready," he murmurs against my heated skin. "Always mine."

"Forever," I reply breathily, but anything else is lost to me as he thrusts forward, slamming his dick inside me, all the way.

"Fuck," I hiss, bracing myself against the wall as water rains down on us from the showerhead.

Luca is relentlessly delicious, pounding into me over and over again. There's nothing for me to do but hold myself up and enjoy the fucking I never have to complain about.

His hand reaches around my front, tweaking each of my nipples until they pebble from his touch, then moves his fingers further south without slowing his pace.

He rubs circles over my clit with his middle finger as he kisses my spine. "You did say a quicky, right?"

I'm panting from the perfect torture only he can provide as I nod, nearly falling over my favorite cliff.

His other hand grips my left hip, pulling me back and helping to keep my head from hitting the tile as he continues to drive into me, allowing his cock to come nearly all the way out before slamming it back in.

My moans grow louder, and I beg Luca for more, knowing only his touch will bring me the euphoria I seek.

He holds both of my hips now and increases his

speed. "You dirty little whore. You just can't ever get enough."

Oh, fuck. This new thing he has with calling me his "little whore" is the oddest turn on, but I eat up his words. Plus, he's not wrong. I can't get enough of him, and I don't think I ever will. No matter how many times he fucks me, I will always want his cock.

Soon, I'm crying out, and black spots dot my vision while I struggle to keep myself upright. Three solid fuckings within twelve hours may have been too much when I'm supposed to be having a girls' day, but I also don't really care if they want to make fun of me for not being able to walk right later.

It'll be worth every crude joke that leaves Justine's mouth.

Luca shudders behind me as tremors rock both of our bodies to their cores, and he pulls me up until my back is flush with his chest. His fingers grip my chin, turning my head until he can kiss me.

"I'm going to miss you today," he whispers against my lips.

My heart constricts with happiness. This man, capable of destruction in so many ways, who puts the fear of God in nearly everyone he encounters...is going to miss me.

Though, what fills me with all the love I have for him is that he no longer hides his true feelings from me. He is open and honest with not only his affection but the rest of his life, including the mafia and Monroe Investments.

Knowing I've broken down his barriers brings me a joy I could never properly describe, and I'm so fucking thankful he chose me and I wake up next to him every day.

I turn and wrap my arms around his neck, smiling up at him with adoration pouring out of me. "Not as much as I'll miss you, but you need to go before I'm late."

He glowers, pressing his forehead against mine. "You only stay for my cock, don't you?"

"Possibly," I tease before stepping back under the spray of water. "Now, let me wash up. I'm already not going to walk right. Don't make me smell like sex, too."

The smirk on his face has me thinking he's going to come back for round two, but he opens the shower door and nods his head. "I don't need anyone else taking an interest in you, so having you walk funny is enough."

I splash water at him, but he's already closed the door and grabbed his towel.

The amount of love I have for that man should be a sin, but I revel in it every day, knowing that because of him, I'm growing into the woman I truly believe I was always meant to be. I've found my place in this world, and I'm surrounded by people who love and respect me.

As I close my eyes and rinse my hair, I can only hope my mother would be proud of all the decisions I've made since her passing.

———

Sitting at brunch with my two best friends, I can't stop from smiling. Tori has been staying at the compound while we make plans to finish up at my mom's house, which I intend to give her.

As much as I envisioned living there and replanting her garden, that dream has shifted. Luca promises to move us to a bigger house with a proper yard, room enough to plant all the things, but finding the perfect place near enough to Portland that will hold all of us isn't as easy as I hoped it would be.

Still, I'm more than content for now, especially since Tori has been more accepting of things ever since I killed Titan. I expected her to push away from me, but if anything, we've grown closer. Though, I can tell there's something still bothering her. I just don't know what yet.

"Did you see Damon this morning?" Justine asks. I shake my head, not realizing he had been released from bedrest already. "He was with Jaxon, taking a stroll through the house."

Damon took a bullet to his hip, shattering the bone. Nobody realized it until the next day, and he was rushed to the hospital for emergency surgery. He also ended up getting an infection in his blood, which kept him down much longer than anticipated.

While he's been expected to make a full recovery this whole time, it's a relief to hear he finally left his room.

"I'm glad to hear it," I say, then nudge Tori. "Want to join me to go check on him later?"

She's distracted with something on her phone, worry

lines forming between her brows, and doesn't reply. When I try to see the screen, she locks her phone. "Huh?"

"What's going on with you?" I ask, reaching for her hand.

She forces a smile to her face and says, "Nothing. That was just work. They're wondering when I'll be back from my family leave."

She's lying through her teeth, but I decide not to call her out on it while we're supposed to be having a good time. I'll force whatever she's concerned with out of her soon.

"Why don't you just quit and work for Monroe like little miss VP over there?" Justine teases and winks at me even though she's talking to Tori.

Yes, Luca gave me an accounting job with a ridiculous title of Vice President, but I told him I wasn't going to work there as a VP until I felt I'd earned the position. My first day will be next week, and I'm eagerly looking forward to putting my degree to real use.

It's not quite the same as having my own accounting firm like I was working toward before, but I have a feeling it might just be even better. Imagining lunches with Luca, fucking on his desk at work... Yeah, that's living the dream.

Nothing will ever be perfect, but I'm pretty sure this is as close as one person can get. I have my friends, my new family, my health, and a man who would literally kill for me.

What more could a girl ask for?

———

Thank you so much for reading the Veiled Vengeance duet! I hope you enjoyed reading Olivia and Luca's story as much as I did writing it!

And if you missed it before, here's your chance to check out Justine and Jaxon's beginning for free right HERE.

ALSO BY THE AUTHORS

Contemporary Romance books as Harper Reed:

The Unexpected Series

A Spicy RomCom trilogy featuring three best friends and their happily-ever-afters!

A Mutually Beneficial Proposal

A Mutually Beneficial Mistake

A Mutually Beneficial Secret

Standalones

A Royal Oops

A Spicy RomCom with royal antics, an epic second chance romance, and a kingdom that needs their new queen.

Paranormal Romance books as Heather Renee:

Mystics and Mayhem World—Series are connected by characters crossovers, but not the plots. You can read them in any order.

Broken Court

A complete New Adult Urban Fantasy series featuring an unconventional and anti-heroine leading lady, a broody love interest, and a fae kingdom with a vile king.

Luna Marked

A complete New Adult wolf shifter series (dual POV) featuring a strong-willed leading lady and a patient, yet fierce alpha male.

Scorned by Blood

A complete New Adult Vampire series featuring a supernatural hunter and the sexy vampire bound to protect her no matter the cost.

Fated to the Wolf

A complete New Adult Witch and Wolf series (dual POV) featuring an abandoned witch, a rogue wolf, and their broken bond.

The Hidden Realm

A complete New Adult wolf and dragon shifter series (dual POV) featuring a feisty wolf shifter just looking for her freedom and a broody dragon trying to save his world.

Individual Series

Raven Point Pack Series

A complete Upper Young Adult Paranormal Romance series featuring wolves, witches, vengeance, and fated mates.

Shadow Veil Academy

A complete Upper Young Adult Urban Fantasy Academy series featuring shifters, elves, witches, and more.

Elite Supernatural Trackers

A complete New Adult Urban Fantasy series featuring witches, demons, a smart-mouthed female lead, alpha males, and a snarky fairy sidekick.

Royal Fae Guardians

A complete Young Adult Urban Fantasy series featuring fae, magic users, a sweet romance, along with snark and humor.

Blood of the Sea Series

A complete Young Adult Paranormal Romance series featuring vampires, open seas adventures, and the occasional pirate.

Standalone Books

Ignite Me - A spicy wolf shifter story featuring a lost heir, the mate who doesn't want her, and the enemies who wish them dead.

Marked Paradox - A Young Adult fae story about a realm divided and one fae to bring them back together.

ABOUT THE AUTHORS

Heather Renee and Harper Reed are actually one in the same. Under Heather Renee, I write slow burn Paranormal Romance and with Harper Reed I get to let loose with steamier contemporary romance. The second name is just so readers can easily identify the varying genres.

My love of reading eventually led to the passion of writing and giving the gift of escapism. When I'm not chatting with the voices in my head, you can usually find me spending time with my family, going on our own adventures, or curled up on the couch with a good book!

If you want to learn more about my books or hang out with me on social media, you can find me in the following places:

For Heather Renee

Newsletter—Reader Group—Facebook Page—Instagram —TikTok—Website—Amazon—Bookbub

For Harper Reed

Reader Group—Facebook Page—Instagram—TikTok— Website—Amazon—Bookbub

www.ingramcontent.com/pod-product-compliance
Lightning Source LLC
Chambersburg PA
CBHW030848200726
48285CB00007B/2600